DUHCAT, MYSTERY and LEGEND UNFOLD

Allen Dionne

Books by Allen Dionne
FICTION

The Seeding Seven's Vision
The Seeding II Virgin Landfall
Duhcat, Mystery and Legend Unfold
A Summer in Mussel Shoals

Cover: Dave Archer painting "Serendipities Portal"
Copyright ©1996
Copyright ©2012 AD by Allen Dionne
Edited by First Editing

Cover design, interior and ebook layout by Integrative Ink.
My deepest thanks to Stephanee Killen:
Integrative Ink's Project Manager

ISBN: 978-0-9853979-2-0

DUHCAT, MYSTERY and LEGEND UNFOLD
is entirely a work of fiction.
Names, characters, places, and incidents are a product of the author's imagination and dreams.
Any similarities to the real world, people, places, and things is purely coincidental.

Printed in the United States of America

For Lily

Dark of night, velvety blackness spangled,
Wonders delved, in countless minds,
Throughout Time

For those who dream of what should be

ONE

Enricco Duhcat was born of parents who were well into their middle age. Their first child came as a very welcome surprise, since they had given up on having children many years before when none had come naturally.

The Duhcats were an old-fashioned family of considerable note. They had no part in elite circles, nor were they of royal blood, but they were incredibly wealthy by measurable standards of the day. All Duhcat children were brought up with the age-old adage that a person is only as good as their word. Good investments, sound family character, and few children meant that an amassed fortune had passed on from one generation to the next. The best solicitors of the day were employed to shelter and protect the family's wealth, which had been building up for five generations through many varied and respectable ventures.

As a very young child not even weaned, Enricco would often gaze into the evening sky. It was stunningly apparent to his parents that he was in extreme awe of the many spangled and twinkling lights.

Shortly after his second birthday, he was already talking more like a grown up than a nursing babe, and he asked his mother what the evening sky's lights were.

"They are stars, my curious one," she answered.

"What are stars? What is the Universe? Are there other people living up there? Can I go and see them?"

To each answer, there came another question—not the normal toddlers "whys" but detailed inquiries and investigations. They could only be explained as the behavior of a savant, or more likely a reborn soul who had stored away spiritual memory of previous travels. He possessed, within his being, an unending fascination towards the mysteries of the evening sky.

As Enricco made way into his second year, his hair grew long, black and full of curls that were not complete circles but the wavy kind, full of body and shiny as raven's wings. His eyes were vast whirlpools of deep brown, flecked with highlights the color of sun-bleached straw. Everyone commented on their spectacular appearance. Young girls swooned. No one had seen such eyes before.

Enricco's precocious and ever-intelligent questions kept the doting parents constantly on their toes. There was never any chance that the child would accept the usual lazy answers most parents give when worn out by a toddler's unending interrogations.

It was as though this child, at the age of two, possessed a brain so developed that it could store, analyze, and interpret data faster than a mere human could verbally impart the same information.

Of course, as with all new parents, his father and mother were in seventh heaven and tended to Ricci—as they had affectionately nick-named him—as though he were a prince.

The lad's character was shown true when even under extreme and smothering attention, and despite the unending patience of both parents and many servants, he never became self-centered or spoke a word to inflate himself or demean another person. Without exception, everyone he came into contact with loved Enricco as if he were their own child.

Innocence, along with an unquenchable thirst for knowledge, appeared to drive Enricco towards a future no one could imagine.

TWO

Long before Enricco's third birthday, he requested a telescope, books, and celestial charts so that he could study. His father asked him what it was that he wanted to study. The boy said simply that he wanted to become familiar with the places he planned to visit when he grew old enough. Not wanting to dampen the boy's curious spirit or dissuade him from his dreams, father and mother took Enricco out shopping.

The child was not satisfied with inexpensive instrumentation. He said simply, "Mother and Father, what need have I of a telescope that will only magnify things I can already see? I have need of seeing things that, at present, I cannot!"

The Duhcat parents obliged and spent what an affluent university would on astronomy equipment to satisfy the most demanding of scholars. They also purchased a mountaintop property so the glare of populous artificial lighting at lower altitudes would not diminish visibility.

After giving up their usual home to be situated on the mountain, the three were never more happy, despite having to brave the snow and being isolated from society for long months during winter. Enricco was the proverbial sponge, soaking up wonders not available to him before. At the age of five, he could expound in detail upon the birth and death of a nova; the ever-present fact that the Universe was expanding; and that, with the present technology, star travel was impossible for a mere human.

It was then that his genius was called to task. As a young boy of six years, he was determined to break the barrier that kept mortal man from moving back and forth through the Universe; he dreamed of and was determined to find a way.

Enricco's parents, instead of scoffing and discouraging him, told him that anything was possible, that the world today would seem impossible to someone born two hundred years ago, and that many believed other far-distant cultures traveled the stars and, in times past, had visited their home planet: Earth.

The boy, driven before by curiosity, was now consumed by two quests: to discover the hidden keys to longevity, and to research quantum physics with the aim of making Deep Space jumps possible in moments rather than over hundreds of light years.

The science of the day told him to give up and that his dreams were impossible...and that to pursue such folly would certainly be a monumental waste of time and resources. But Enricco believed fervently that *anything* was possible. He continued his quest, undaunted by the ingrained limitations spewed forth by the best scientists and astral physicists of the day. Enricco continued, untrammeled by the vast and varied boundaries set by the respected minds of the era and by those who had gone before.

Enricco's parents, feeling the boy was spending too much time in his research and studies, began an astronomy camp for young, brilliant minds. Enricco had not desired to spend time in socializing, being all consumed by his dreams, so his parents brought a social network to the boy. The mountain could not easily be brought down into society and culture, so humanity was brought up to the mountain.

The camp drew young people from the far reaches of Earth. A swimming pool was built, walking trails improved, cabins erected, and playfields maintained for outdoor sports. A few select teachers were brought in to educate the children in areas of specialized knowledge.

Enricco at first seemed put out by the idea of sharing his mountaintop, but his father and mother would not be dissuaded. In the end, the astronomy camp was a huge success. Applications continued coming in, and soon there were many more applicants than space permitted students.

Thus, Enricco grew up in association with the brightest young minds available. The creative energy and drive of the children became a catalyst for inspired thinking in the young boy's mind. He grew tall, not confined to his own intellect alone, and he experienced diverse and inexhaustible streams of perspectives, which stimulated his intellect and moved him into exciting and startlingly new directions.

As the years passed, Enricco excelled in sports. He became an avid rock climber (much to his mother's chagrin), fished the streams, hunted wild rabbit and game fowl, and toughened his body climbing and biking the many steep trails, all of which led to views, unobstructed and vast.

Enricco's love of the outdoors was only surpassed by his dream of Deep Space travel. The many girls and subsequently young women who came to Camp Magellan were enthralled when they were fortunate enough to gather in Enricco's grasp of the Universe seen from the observatory, and his personal points of view. They were not only impressed by his grasp of astral physics, relative time, dimensional space tiers, Deep Space warping, and the potential for dream-sleep projection; they were also enamored of his mild manner; exquisite, exotic physical appearance; generous heart; and the fact he was one of the wealthiest, most progressive, unattached young men of his day

People who knew him at the time did not fully understand his obsession. All children have dreams, yet many times—if not most times—the youthful aspirations are waylaid, marriage comes, and then children, along with the numerous and joyful responsibilities that make up our lives. Childhood dreams are forgotten or relegated to the back of our minds. Momentary reflections and longings come later in life, when not a person alive fails to ask themselves whether the choices that have directed their course up to the present were properly chosen. Not with Enricco; never did doubt creep in, nor did he falter in the faith he held.

Many of the best schools granted Enricco full scholarships. Planetary government prodigy programs clamored to enlist the young man. Enricco resolved to tread his own path, to search out answers that came not from organized education or religion but from the divinely inspired depth of his own unique and enquiring soul.

The path he had chosen as a young boy would not be altered – not by beautiful intelligent young women, not by a government that offered many luring programs, and not even by his parents, who, like most loving fathers and mothers, wished to see grandchildren running about the house.

THREE

Enricco Duhcat, dedicated to a dream, worked eighteen hours a day. Undistracted by ego, the ever-present pitfalls of young love, lack of money, or undue and unwanted spiritual influence, he thrived and grew in physical stature and in mental and spiritual clarity. Inspiration flashed to Enricco on many occasions, and before long, he had tapped into a vein available to all of us who believe: search unselfishly, work honestly, strive diligently, and travel a chosen path without allowing doubt to erode faith. A stream of inspiration will often present the missing pieces to almost any puzzle that is being painstakingly assembled.

Enricco learned this truth early on. His wisdom and intellect, truly much more than remarkable, flourished. Knowledge infused his being, as momentary flashes of brilliant light opened doors and cast rays of illumination upon otherwise dark corners of confusion and nagging doubt.

The secret to Enricco successfully accomplishing what was previously thought impossible by the foremost scientists of the time lay within the inspired creativity he tapped.

And tap he did, with such fervor that his home planet developed the ability to travel Deep Space, only after he unencrypted the keys he had hidden, nearly two centuries later.

On an astonishing spring day, after scaling Blue Bend's sheer face freehand—which was previously thought to be impossible—he stood on the eleven hundred foot high vertical face, reciting poetry to the distant horizon. Then, it came like lightning: a dawning the magnitude of which would take two centuries for Earth and its inhabitants to comprehend. Enricco gathered in divine inspiration as a fisherman brings in a net full of precious bounty.

Dazed from the light in his brain, he stumbled into a thicket. His foot met only air, and he slid into a dark crevasse that had been hidden by the thick, brushy growth on the top of the sheer cliff face.

Revealed to him in the meager light of the shaft was a vast cavern, previously undiscovered. Enricco knew instantly that his finding of the cavern and the astonishing inspiration were intertwined, and that here, in this secret location, he would build the vessel that would take him throughout the stars.

He resolved in that instant to speak with his parents about funding his dream.

FOUR

"Enricco, the cornerstone of all true worth is measured, weighed, and set with a mortar composed of truth," Enricco's father, Anton Duhcat said. "A nobility which bestows kindness and generosity on the less fortunate, and that leads one to forget desires for material wealth and personal security."

Anton Duhcat stooped and picked up a small stone then threw it into the water, it sent ripples in all directions.

"One's heart drives the conscious body, not the calculations of the human mind, which are fraught with caprice, varying moods, and shifting tides. If you promise me that your work will encompass the cornerstone of which I have just spoken, I will acquiesce to your needs and offer all that we hold: our good thoughts, our love for you, the family's fortunes, and more."

"Dad, you and Mom have always believed in me. I don't think for a second that any of this would have been possible without your loving help throughout my young life. Now, with a breathtaking flash of inspiration in front of us, you give all. Thank you. I am overwhelmed."

The young man went to his beloved father and, in a common show of affection between the two, embraced him. "Can I break the exciting news to Mom?"

"Son, can it really be done?"

"Sir, with the inspiration I received from a source vastly higher than my own intellect, I have no doubt it can."

"And when you have conquered the mystery of traveling the stars, what will be next for you?"

"I wish to give the common man places of refuge. I desire to form some sort of protection for them...a society or culture that offers not only security but also the opportunity every human *should* have to be truly creative and free from transparent bondage. As I see it, Father, Earth has become a home for worker ants—or bees, if you will—who are quickly worn out and replaced by a new generation of the same; meanwhile, a handful of greedy, callous, and mostly evil billionaires siphon the profits from the lifetime of toils of each dying generation."

Enricco stopped speaking for a momen. He looked out to the horizon as if gathering his thoughts. Brushing one hand threw his dark wavy hair, he continued.

"People are so caught up in the machine that consumes them that little is left but the daily labor necessary to provide themselves with food, shelter, and clothing. Few indeed have the stamina to rise above the trap set by the wealthy, who become more powerful and greedy with each generation that passes. In the future, I see a system of governance that precludes certain types of persons from gaining the stranglehold they have affected here on Earth."

"How is that to be accomplished?" his father asked, with questioning eyes.

"The answer to your question evades me at the moment. I have only ever touched upon it in fleeting thoughts, or in the dreams that pass through my mind while I sleep. Now my entire focus and energy must be directed on the ship, which will be the vehicle able to transport us from this beautiful planet that I love, but which has become something saddening my heart. We will have a new beginning: that *is* the fresh dream I have just shared with you."

"These things of which you speak, son, are noble and just, not to mention mindboggling. We will do what we can to help."

"Father, what I have shared with you must remain strictly between us; no one can know of the project's existence or of my goals. Do you understand?"

"You have my word; it will be as you wish. When do you begin?"

"I have chosen the spot for the ship to be constructed. The area needs to be cleared and made ready. I await the necessary funds to begin."

"They are yours. I will make the arrangements today, and you will have full, unfettered access to all funds needed. You have some understanding of the family assets; will it be enough?"

"Yes, Father, but there will be little left; however, the family fortune will be replenished quickly by those who wish to migrate elsewhere, for the passage will bear an expense to each migrant that is equal to the value of this trip to freedom."

FIVE

The university president read the report with subdued interest. A young man not yet nineteen years of age had just finished challenging final exams over a broad realm of science, but with a particular focus on astral and quantum physics. The results were astounding: each and every final had been the accumulated knowledge of a completed doctorate. The scores were perfect.

The tests had been conducted with hidden surveillance gear that monitored the students to insure there could be no outside assistance or hidden notes. The disconcerting thing was that in his thesis, the young man had postulated theories that went contrary to the view of the league of minds in power in the community of astral physics. Could it be, the president wondered, that this young man by the name of Enricco Duhcat had stumbled onto something that, if accepted, would set the reigning community of science on its head?

He remembered that some years back, this same Duhcat had flatly turned down a full scholarship to the university, along with numerous similar offers from an assortment of the most prestigious schools operating advanced astral physics programs.

Rumor had it that Earth's government had attempted to enlist him in the top-secret research and development Prodigy Program. This offer was politely declined as well. Now, without any known formal education, the young man had aced a wide gambit of final exams and thus had qualified for a multiple doctorate at the tender age of nineteen. This type of accomplishment was unheard of, yet the results and subsequent report validating them were staring the president boldly in the face.

Clear policy dictated that the president forward the results to proper channels in government; after all, minds like this were highly sought after for secret research and development programs in Deep Space and in weapons development programs.

After compiling the data, the university president shrugged his shoulders, chalked it up to a very enlightening read, and bounced the full report to the proper government department.

He wished the young man well in whatever path he chose. *I take my hat off to another brilliant young mind,* he thought.

SIX

Within the hardened facility, deeply buried beneath an otherwise nondescript mountain, the meeting began. Present were some of the top government minds in science and in the military's Space Research Program.

"Shall we begin?" the chair asked.

Consent was nodded around the table.

"If you would, Doctor, being our foremost authority on these subjects, I would appreciate your opinion. Of course, you have been given time to study and consult with your colleagues on the matter. What does the group of you think?"

"We are of like mind on this very interesting dissertation. There is no doubt among us that this Duhcat is a brilliant young man; he has attained the highest scores ever recorded within the walls of the testing institution. A new academic record has been set across a wide realm of subjects. It is our understanding that these scores have not been matched at any other educational institutions either.

"However, with regards to his doctoral dissertation and its *fantastic* theories, we will draw the line. The premises of our sciences have long been established and proven, since time immemorial. The foundation of our creed has been backed up by the beliefs and educational background of many respected and renowned scientists: those who have been ordained through time as the foundations and the cornerstones that hold up the great architecture of modern physics and science. They have been, and still are, a veritable treasure trove—a concert, if you will allow me the analogy, of extraordinarily brilliant intellects of the past and present.

Doctor Knobson scratched at the side of his tacky hairpiece, as he gathered his thoughts.

"Are we to believe this young man is so mentally well-endowed that we should take his imaginations as concrete fact and upset the foundations of our science, which have been in place for centuries? We think not! While he is obviously brilliant, he is also a renegade! He breaks from tradition! He literally spits on what we have all spent our lives studying, as if his theories were the Holy Grail!

"The work of the masters, those who went before us and those who still slave daily with meager rewards, who work to see the fruition of dreams once held, will not be turned over so easily. These people are now forging and tempering the principles of science, a science that is, I might add, based on results—not abject theories and speculations.

"Even if funding were granted—and we think that would be a waste of time and money—the theories in his dissertation would take decades to investigate, test, prove, and then implement in real-world time, space, and physics, assuming there was even any merit in the fantastic assumptions he takes liberty in presenting as foundationally based FACT! All the while, OUR path would be seriously injured by moving the necessary personnel and funds to support such a preposterous endeavor. The progress made, by dire sacrifice and loss of family time by our team, would be seriously jeopardized by creating another school of thought that runs contrary to the designs we see coming into fruition, and *soon!*

"This Duhcat's theories are a proverbial Ouija board of discontent. If High Command has any true hope, any real dream of traveling the stars, that hope should not be instilled in this upstart, Enricco Duhcat!"

"Thank you, Professor. To be clear, are you all in agreement as a group? There are no other points of view?"

All heads, which housed the closed-minded brains of the creative-science program, nodded in unison.

"Very well. We appreciate your point of view on this interesting doctoral thesis. Thank you, that will be all."

The stiff-minded academics rose from their seats, and, with bent shoulders and shuffling feet, left the conference.

The military leaders remained. Silence pervaded the group of twelve for a time, while they each pondered the enigma of Enricco Duhcat.

One of the group finally spoke: "Freakin' stuffed shirts!"

Another commented comically, "Don't mess with my belief system; I wouldn't know how to handle that!"

The chair of the twelve said, "All right, enough nonsense. This matter requires our utmost attention."

The room quieted.

The general began speaking.

"We have plugged these theories of Duhcat's into the master military computer. All this computer does is to promulgate them further—no roadblocks, no holes, no faults. I think it deserves consideration. While the computer hit the end of the trail, so to speak, it has not shown anything that would toss these theories into the garbage as quickly as our esteemed scientific colleagues desire to do!"

"Well, sir," the youngest at the table said. "We all know of the *unlimited* funding that is pouring fourth like a never-ending waterfall to those closed-minded geeks. If Duhcat's ideas have substance, they know that power and resources for them will be diminished, and Duhcat would become the star-studded child of a new era; they would be the washed up has-beens soon to be placed on waivers. Their resistance is natural to human nature. However, Earth is *not* flat, as was once believed. It is an accepted fact that it is a sphere…we now know the truth. What if Duhcat's theories are being looked at in the same dysfunctional way? I mean, these guys are supposed to be the cutting edge, but they don't want to follow the possibilities? I think our cutting edge has been dulled by cloistered thinking. I think we need a breath of fresh air, and I think Duhcat is the wind bringing it. Does anyone here know the story of Jack Kilby?"

No one in the room commented.

"In 1958, Jack Kilby was a young electrical engineer who had previously been denied entrance to MIT because he failed the entrance exam by three points. The Army, Navy, Air Force, and the forerunner to NASA had all implemented research sections for a project whose aim was first to minimize the millions of wires and bulky components necessary to construct a computer that would not generate excessive or crippling heat; and second, to reduce the computer in size so that it could be used in aircraft, ground vehicles, and, someday, space. The problems were monumental, and billions were thrown at solving them. No one could. At least, not until Jack Kilby came along.

"This guy was awarded the Nobel Prize for Science. He invented the first super-conducting micro-chip. So...a green young guy who couldn't even get into MIT was responsible for a breakthrough in technology that billions in government money had been unable to spawn! Years later, when Kilby was asked to what he attributed his success, he said something to the effect of—and I am not quoting exactly here—'I was young and green; I was thinking out of the box, and anything was possible. So, by not discounting anything, I wasn't held back by engrained beliefs and thought patterns.' Don't you all see?"

"Your refreshing viewpoint makes sense to me," said General Armstrong. "Other comments?"

"He is right," another said. "If we don't attempt to follow different avenues of research and development, but instead place all our faith in the group that just left, I believe it would be a grave mistake. What if Duhcat is correct? What if the theories continue to hold water?"

Others in the group nodded agreement.

"Do we have at least a quorum then?"

Hands rose; consent was unanimous.

"Good!" said the general. "We will stay with Duhcat's side. We will wait, watch, learn, and implement. We will pick up the ball, so to speak, and carry it far as possible."

"Sir?" It was the youngest speaking once more. "In my opinion, we will need a separate group of scientists, different from those who have rejected the possibilities. We would need another facility as well, to avoid mixing between the groups. The directive should be an island unto itself, with no cross contamination of doctrine. We need fresh insight, and young bright minds. I have some contacts I can tap for the people necessary." Cobran thought about Camp Magellan's roster of students and one in particular who was *very* close to Duhcat.

"All right, Cobran, you have the con on this one. Your sentiments parallel my own. Hell, this Duhcat's test scores make our guys look like they should all be wearing dunce caps, and he's never even *attended* formal schooling."

"Sir, with all due respect, our school system would often look at a prodigy like Duhcat as a non-conformist freak…a rule breaker. No wonder our group of eggheads want to thrash his theories; they've spent their entire lives in that system and were trained to look at things a certain way. Duhcat doesn't have that inherent handicap. We certainly understand and acknowledge that inspiration has been the key to many breakthrough technologies in the past; we should keep that in the forefront of our minds with this one. Sir, to see this through, I'm going to need an assistant to share a bit of the workload. Will you authorize that?"

"Of course, Cobran. We are placing this as top priority. You are to monitor Duhcat, enlist the necessary people who are qualified, and if his ideas seem to pan out, position us there to catch the bounty. Understood?"

"Yes, sir!"

SEVEN

Cobran left the meeting absorbed in thought. The premise of Duhcat's thesis was intended to disrupt the status quo. It was obvious to a techno geek like Cobran that Duhcat's thesis was intended to open investigating minds to new possibilities, things that could not necessarily be proven on a chalkboard by a physicist.

No wonder these entrenched scientists were having trouble, he thought. The worst part was that they wouldn't even consider the application of his theories; they were just throwing them by the wayside and hoping they would not come back to haunt their rigid, disciplined processes further.

He entered his small, cluttered, suffocating office, looked around, and thought that today had just dropped a brilliant beam of sunlight upon his shoulders. Cobran visualized his new office: one with some windows for a change, a staff of his own, and the healthy salary increase that naturally came with upper management positions. He was the general's most recent golden child. Cobran promised himself that he would make the most of it while the blessing lasted.

He thought of Sabrina, and how she had smiled at him when they met in the halls. Could he pry her away from the administrative treadmill she was on and use her as an executive secretary? He thought the idea had merit; why not have a beautiful assistant instead of the old hags with whom he was normally stuck.

Cobran smiled to himself as he left his dinky office and walked towards Sabrina's desk.

Sabrina sat in a bit of sunlight shining in through the window, which illuminated her strawberry blonde hair.

"Good morning, gorgeous!" he said, smiling.

"What's up, Cobran?"

So cool, he thought. *Nothing but business.* Hoping that might change, he replied, "Big promotion: a new project. Could we have lunch together? I'll fill you in."

"I'm swamped! People have been dumping on my desk all morning. Sometimes I wonder what they do all day! I think they figure I will do *their* work, while *they* go for a two-hour cocktail lunch. I was going to work through lunch and try to catch up. Sometimes it's the only period in the day where I have an hour without constant interruptions."

She quit talking and looked at him.

Cobran wondered whether she was thinking that *he* was another distraction. "Sabrina, I have a thought. How would you like to be promoted to executive secretary? Twice the salary, your own assistant, a nice big office instead of this cubicle. What do you think?"

"I think you've lost your mind. I've been stuck at this desk for two years, and the better I get at my job, the more work they pile on. It's a vicious circle."

"So your answer is yes?"

"Yes to what?"

"To lunch!"

"I don't think so, Cobran," she said, shaking her head. "I have my desk to clear before I can feel good about going home."

"Oh, I guess you didn't hear. I'm offering you a promotion, and a new office. We'll probably have to travel a bit for surveillance reasons. Nice hotels, an unfettered expense account, double time on holidays."

"You're joking right? You, Cobran, *have* obviously lost your mind. No minion rises through the ranks as quickly as that!"

"Absolutely not. My mind is sound. I've been authorized by the general to form a team. You are my first draft pick."

Sabrina looked at him closely. The all-business seriousness moved her, and her face softened. She smiled genuinely and said, "What do you want from me...in trade for all that?"

"Right now, I want you to come to lunch. If you agree with my proposal, I'll run it by the general and see if he will authorize your transfer."

She grabbed her purse and then stood, pushing her chair back in place. Looking coolly into his eyes as if searching for some trick, she said, "I'm all yours."

EIGHT

Duhcat sensed the energy. Subtle shifts had taken place not long after he had successfully challenged a series of doctoral exam finals. Intuitively, he knew. He began preparations, taking all necessary precautions to cloak his work beneath the surface of camouflage netting.

Duhcat built his shop and lab above the fissure that led to the secret cavern. He made provision for secret access to the chamber far below, while above ground he created a misleading smokescreen for the government. He would appear to be above ground doing the work. Programs would be written. Alloy and composites would be shaped into a ship. A small, model-sized prototype of a Deep Space craft would be built, and complicated computer programs, based on theories about Deep Space jumps, would be written and stored in its computers. These files hackers would be *allowed* to access, all as a false trail: a ruse to keep listening ears and eyes away from the real designs taking shape deep inside Blue Bend's sheer limestone cliff.

The shop section of the lab had been built on top of a twenty-four-inch thick concrete slab. The concrete floor was webbed and reinforced with fifteen tons of high-grade steel bar. Thin lead sheeting had been laid beneath the soil where the floor would be poured to block x-ray equipment's prying eyes. Half the concrete slab was supported in a vertical channel by multiple and massive hydraulic rams that would, when activated, lower the slab and expose the entrance to his real work far below.

Once the lab was completed, Duhcat focused on the real project: his ship.

Far beneath the surface, the vessel took shape slowly. Working alone with exacting care, Enricco reproduced the flashing visions that had inspired the work months running into years before.

Above ground, in the lab, he took the same care in designing another ship and drive system, one that, upon first investigation, appeared to fulfill all the necessary requirements for space travel yet fell far short of the expectation prying eyes desired.

Silently, he named the mirage ship *False Trails*.

Monitoring his communication system and the property surrounding the lab, he soon noticed a pattern of intrusion, not by flesh and blood but by sophisticated electronic spyware only available to secret-ops divisions of government. His intuition had been correct: they were watching.

Duhcat went to great lengths to mask his movements. He built a replica of himself that mimicked his natural movements at the computers and at the complicated electronic control board. The dummy was internally heated to 98.6 degrees Fahrenheit. He would place Junior, as he called the drone, at the keyboard and enact a simple program that would run as though a live person were using the computer to write complicated programming dialogs.

Drawing the shades remotely to let natural light into the lab, he would appear for half of the day and part of the night, hammering away, stroking the keyboard. In real time, Duhcat was far beneath the surface, accomplishing the secret project unnoticed, although he spent some time each day working on *False Trails*. Progress was slow but steady on both ships.

Soon, as Duhcat appeared to be nearing completion of *False Trails* and the Deep Space drive mechanism that would never actually be able to power the decoy ship, the electronic eavesdropping became intense and the intrusions doubled in frequency.

NINE

"You see, Sabrina, there is a young man by the name of Enricco Duhcat, who wrote his Doctoral Thesis on astral physics, focusing on theoretical Deep Space jumps. Keep in mind, this guy is nineteen and has never been to school. Well, to shorten the story, his theories go completely against the path our best scientists are following and have been for over one hundred and fifty years, but our scientists have never actually come up with any realistic answers for how to cover the vast distances of Deep Space with the propulsion systems they are using and the time that allows. The only solution they've come up with is deep sleep, but the complications *that* causes are horrendous. It's an asinine concept to begin with, yet our government, under the direction of these eggheads, has spent countless fortunes attempting to solve the never-ending problems."

Cobran stopped speaking for a moment and took a drink of water from his glass.

"Then along comes Duhcat. He challenges the status quo and, in doing so, all these entrenched scientists feel threatened and want to do nothing but trashcan his theories. Yet the master military computer has run his theories repeatedly and has found no holes, no faults. Of course, we don't have the all the answers. Undoubtedly, Duhcat is working on them as we speak.

"That is my new designation: I am to monitor Duhcat; gather a separate research team; organize a new facility; and clandestinely track his work, hack his systems, and keep abreast of his progress. We hope that, in time, we can extract the secret of momentary Deep Space jumps. Don't you see? It would open up the Universe to our government and to our culture."

"Are you so sure, Cobran, that if we were successful, the result of our piracy would be a good thing?" Sabrina asked.

Cobran's excitement stalled. His face went blank for a moment. Then he said, "Sabrina...this designation means I have been given carte blanche.... Am I to pass up an extraordinary opportunity like this? The moral rights and wrongs of the situation aren't ours to decide. Where Duhcat's potential technology may be focused, if it ever comes to fruition, isn't either."

"I just wondered about *your* thoughts, Cobran," she said, shrugging. "Count me in. I could use a change of pace and a bit of fresh air. Did you say we would be spending some time in the mountains?"

Cobran nodded. "Lots of time, actually. We will be up there for at least four days, sometimes five per week. You and I will be the ones collecting the data by keeping close to Duhcat, all without him ever realizing we are watching. The latest in covert-ops tech is ours!"

Sabrina looked closely at Cobran. She had always liked the man but had never thought her job would place her in such an intimately close working environment. She thought about the possibilities and imagined evenings in a cozy cabin in front of a warm, glowing fire and…

"Sounds like a blast," she said. "When do we leave!"

TEN

Duhcat had installed the counter-surveillance gear long before the intrusions began. Expecting the prying eyes of the government, he was well prepared to protect himself and his work. All his equipment had been installed with filters that would baffle the probing electronic devices that would inevitably be looking toward him when the games began.

When the government man named Cobran had begun to place his equipment into play, Duhcat's system of counter surveillance had the man recorded, as well as the locational placement of the many secret-ops devices. Also, when Cobran's executive assistant, Sabrina, began her hacking forays into his family's data bank, Duhcat followed her intrusions with relish. She was obviously attempting to learn more about his sphere of influence and acquaintances.

Enricco didn't like unexpected surprises and was confident he had himself well covered. Nonetheless, he spent a great deal of time writing and then re-writing a non-lethal virus, then hacked into the government's top-secret system and planted it deep in the secret program. It would spread invisibly, piggybacking on groups of binary coding, the foundation of all computer operating systems.

The purpose of the program was not to inflict degradation on the machines it hid within, but rather to transmit to Duhcat's aboveboard computer, without a trace, all information the government program was working on. He then encrypted the data, cleansed it, and copied it to flash drives that were stored in a *not* so secret location. This way, when the government came, as he knew they would, they could only seize what he *wanted* them to seize.

This allowed him to receive the information without them knowing he was tapped in. In this manner, he was kept informed of their information-gathering progress and their attempted implementation of the elaborate smoke screen of data he had allowed them to steal.

ELEVEN

Cobran and Sabrina had been running the operation for over two years. Duhcat appeared to be making slow progress on the formulas, which laid his theories into the real-world realm of astral physics.

The hackers on staff had taken weeks to pass into Duhcat's system, slowly penetrating layer upon layer of encrypted protection. Duhcat was being as careful as a rabbit when the hawk's shadow passes by, yet the advanced methods and looped password programs eventually broke the codes. Before long, the encryption would change, and the process would start over.

Cobran organized the intel and presented it to the elite staff of young prodigies that had been hand-picked for the task. One of Cobran's primary criteria for the candidates was that they must be freethinkers, able to believe in inspired thought and not just in the trudging doldrums that most research-and-development geeks plodded through on a daily basis. Cobran's goal with the program was to break through modes of conformity and choose paths that were as yet untrammeled.

The surveillance became an avenue for him to travel towards two things: he had slowly endeared himself to Sabrina, and they were getting out of the city and into the mountains he had grown to love as a child.

The job's perks were unending. A few hours of monitoring Duhcat's Lair, as Sabrina had affectionately named it, earned them the open door to activities about which most city folk only dreamed. As a child, Cobran's father had often taken him to these very mountains, so he had an affinity for the sheer slopes, glistening glaciers, and fish-filled rivers and lakes. Nature beckoned to him once more. When he was not actually working on the case, his hours were spent enjoying boating, fishing, hiking, and sampling the fine cuisine available at upper-crust eateries that targeted the tourist buck.

Life was good, he thought, as he and Sabrina enjoyed the drive from the city to the higher elevations where their expertise was called upon every week. They would spend a few days on task, fulfilling their appointed duties, and often they would stay the weekend if the crowds were not too thick.

Not long into the venture, Sabrina had softened. The evenings, and many afternoons, were often spent in the warmth of her arms, breathing her savory fragrance and enjoying her delicate touch. In all, Cobran was happier than he'd ever been and wished fervently that Duhcat would take a lifetime finishing and polishing his work.

A few months into the mission, a vacation house had come up empty just across the valley from Blue Bend's sheer face. The elevation was right for use as a vantage point, and the distance was far enough away for their target to be indiscernible and yet close enough to eavesdrop with high-powered gear without complications.

A long-term lease was taken on the home. Sabrina and Cobran set up house. The two enjoyed seemingly endless quiet evenings together, away from the throngs of tourists who flocked to the hills year-round.

The house also gave them the distinct advantage of being able to watch Duhcat's coming and goings without having to travel back and forth from a hotel or skulk in the woods. More than half of each workweek was spent at the house; the other time was spent in the office, taking care of the many details that called their attention.

Duhcat avoided phones like the plague. In fact, he did not have one in his lab. This precluded any phone-tapping to gain more intel and left Cobran and Sabrina to visual monitoring and digital intrusions into his database.

Early into the second year, Sabrina came up with an interesting idea. Sitting at home in the mountains one evening on the covered stone terrace, she expounded on her thoughts. "Duhcat's parents operate an astronomy camp for young people, and they have for years. I have obtained a list of all the people who have attended. What if we recruited one of the young women—one who is not just extremely bright but also very physically desirable? There are quite a few who still keep in contact with him."

"What are your thoughts?" he asked, taking his eyes from the view across the valley. She had piqued his interest.

"Duhcat has no girlfriend. He is certainly at an age when his juices *should* be raging. What if we could find in his correspondences with these girls one who was special, one in whom he might confide, one with whom he shows some inclination to be more than friends?"

"Go on," Cobran said.

"Just say we could recruit that one and tell her that, in the interest of planetary security, we need her help. We could pay her an exorbitant salary, give her the car of her dreams, and a guaranteed retirement."

"And why would we do all that, my dear?"

"So that her loyalties would be with us and not with him, silly," Sabrina said.

"I don't know, Sabrina. From what I've seen of his communications with the women attendees he was acquainted with at Camp Magellan, they all seem to fawn over him. I mean, I can hear the pitter-patter of their longing hearts every time I read the scripts. He seems to draw them like magnets, yet he shows little interest in their intentions. All I see from him is very businesslike, no frills, no romancing. This guy is very different. I know when I was his age, babes were my number one priority; my education came second."

"Not anymore?" she asked, batting her beautiful blue eyes flagrantly.

"You and only you, babe," he said, smiling.

"I'm flattered. I thought you were keeping me around as a convenience."

"You are pretty damn convenient right now." Cobran ran a hand up Sabrina's bare thigh. She stopped him at the hem of her mini and said teasingly, "Bad boy! We are working. What would the general think?"

"Oh dear, you sure know how to bring work crashing into my fantasies."

"Later, I promise," she told him. "Right now, I was trying to stay on track. Will you help? Surely a few more minutes waiting won't kill you."

"A few minutes? As in three?"

She nodded.

"No, I guess you're right," he said, and feigned a pout.

She picked up his hand and placed it back in his own lap.

"Now, where was I? Oh, we recruit one of his friends; she gets close. He confides in her, as all men do in intimate moments, and then we have another perspective:

another entry point. Right now, we don't have a clue how close he is or when the ship will be ready. At least with our confidant on the inside, we could possibly gather some clues as to the progress from Duhcat's perspective and not just from what we find on his computer. After all, what man can help expounding to a beautiful young woman whom he fancies?"

"It might work," said Cobran, deep in thought.

"Sure it will!"

"Do you have anyone particular in mind? Anyone you think he's grown especially fond of?"

"There are a few who I think have potential, yet one in particular strikes me."

"Tell me all about her. I can see by the twinkle in your eyes, you think this vixen has what it takes. Don't you?"

"First of all, she is French."

"That's a good start!"

"Oui oui!" Sabrina began laughing.

"What else, you evil little matchmaker?"

"Well, right after she began attending Camp Magellan, Enricco hired a private tutor. Do you want to guess what he began studying?"

"You know I dislike guessing games. Call me a party pooper."

"French, of course. He began with private lessons, got additional audio-language courses, and inside of a year was speaking the language fluently—grammar, idioms, syntax, context, male and female gender. French is one of the most complicated of the old European languages; learning it that quickly is truly an impossible task."

"Once again, our wonder-boy prevails."

"Sounds like you're jealous."

"Sounds like he gets the girl, while I am left in the cold, freezing. If my teeth were chattering any harder, they'd be full of chips."

"Poor baby!" Sabrina said with mock sympathy, matching his offbeat humor.

"What is this French heartbreaker's name and background?"

"Monique Delante. Graduate of the University of Paris, with honors degrees in astral physics, psychology, and foreign language. She speaks English with no accent, has gone on to a position as Director of Astronomy at the Touraine Facility, keeps in contact with Duhcat almost daily, and often speaks of her love for the United States and for the mountains here in particular. She also never fails to imply her affection in a variety of ways at the end of her communications."

"I think your ideas are great," Cobran said. "I'll run it by the general. We can do that in person on Monday, and then, if he consents, send our potential infiltrator the offer of her dreams. Of course, that offer would have to include her working with the staff we have on project, as well as her clandestine responsibilities."

"Of course! Are you being so agreeable just because you desire some soft favors from me, buddy?"

"I would never stoop so low!" he said, laughing. "Well, on second thought, I might, if that's what it takes to be done working for the day."

"Ah, I see my power, and you keeping this secret for so long! But as for the stop working part, I was hoping you had just begun."

"You can't call this work, Sabrina…"

When the news came in to Enricco that Cobran and Sabrina intended to hire Monique to infiltrate, he found the information humorous and exciting at the same time. He was curious about Monique's loyalty, and the strength of their friendship. *An interesting game begins,* he thought, chuckling at the news.

It was already a game, with him watching them watch him build *False Trails* and the dummy drive system and operating programs. As he worked, he regularly reviewed the listeners' interpretations and evolved his theories, constructing an increasingly elaborate ruse for the benefit of them all. Enricco found no small humor in the game and began to enjoy the play rather than looking upon it as a nuisance consuming his valuable time.

He waited patiently, contemplating the next major move of his adversary: their attempt to hire his childhood friend Monique as an infiltrator to his very private world.

TWELVE

The special courier came, walking up in his neat little uniform. He was shown through security cordons by one of the guards she knew. Monique instantly believed someone was dead.

Mother? Father? Her heart leapt into her throat.

Grasping the envelope from the young man's hand, she spun and walked rapidly away, looking for somewhere she could be alone, to find a niche in which the bad news could be read, received, and contemplated.

The envelope wouldn't open. Her shaking hands were having difficulty finding the tab by which she could strip the ribbon and expose the contents. Her mind raced. No one sent messages like this anymore! *Someone could have called,* she thought. She felt like an actress in an old war movie, receiving news of a husband's death.

Finally, she tore at the envelope, frantically ripping away pieces of the corners to get to the news inside.

The type jumped out at her. *"The United States Government would like you to visit and consider an opportunity in the Prestigious Astral Physics Research and Development Program."*

Monique gasped relief. Not bad news but good, maybe.

She stopped reading for a moment and caught her breath. Her heart was still pounding. She took a few deep breaths and then walked to her office, where she could read the communication in silence.

The letter was short and to the point: the move would be to San Francisco; the position was at the University of Berkley, where she would be working for the U.S. Government's secret facility on campus. The offer was for $245,000 per year, plus a car of her choice, a twenty-year contract, and full retirement at the end of the twenty-year term. It was unbelievable!

The French government was paying her crumbs. She could barely afford gas for the tiny car she used to commute home—when she didn't spend her nights at the installation. The cot in the back room of her miniscule office had grown way too familiar with her impression. Here was a chance—a chance to break free of the stifling job she had landed after eight grueling years of advanced education.

She began laughing hysterically. She was glad to be alone. Tears rolled down her cheeks.

Then it hit her like a brick in the head. *Enricco! Oh my god!* she thought. He was in the mountains of Northern California, just a few hours from where she would be working if she accepted the position.

Ever since she had been a young girl, he had been her fancy. She thought of those huge, swirling, golden-flecked eyes that sparkled electricity when he looked at the stars or spoke of the potential for high-speed Deep Space travel. Her intuitive mind immediately questioned the coincidence of the offer, and the distance it would close between them.

Her desire to see him overpowered relative thought, and she began making plans. She wouldn't tell him; she would surprise him by appearing out of the blue. Her heart raced in anticipation.

She had always been his favorite. All the other girls at the camp had disliked her with passion due to the time he spent alone with her. At times, the two of them had seemed inseparable. Yet, in the end, when the summer had waned, she had been dragged back to France, to her home, to the drudgery of school.

The only thing that had spurred her on was to learn as much as she could while she was away for the school year so that when she returned, he would be proud of how hard she had worked.

She thought of how, when she had first arrived at the camp, they had struggled through the language barrier. Many of the girls spoke English well, but for Monique it had been a hard-won battle. She had started learning the language late in her young life, and she had been frustrated to no end. He had hired a special tutor to teach him French and her English. There had been so many laughs: the confusing of words, the tumbled down phrases, the thoughts that seemed clear but invariably turned out to be an insult or bad word of some sort.

She laughed to herself, remembering how their knowledge of language had merged so that one day, seemingly with the snap of their fingers, they could converse fluidly with no problems at all. They had both gone on to master each other's language. It was their common bond, something they had fought for together, something nothing and no one could ever take away.

Enricco! OH! My! GOD! she thought.

She had built up leave and vacation time and could take a month off. Her assistant could easily handle the workload. In that instant, she made up her mind. She shrieked, jumping in the air, waving her arms and dancing. The music of love's possibilities played in her head, and she knew that her destiny, created by her hard work and sheer resolve, had opened this wonderful window in time. All she had to do was be brave enough to step through, without doubt or trepidation. She believed that they were meant to be near each other, always.

She left the facility without even clearing her computer, got home, packed in an hour, and was at the airport waiting for the first standby seat to any city in the U.S. five hours after the message had arrived.

THIRTEEN

Duhcat broke from his work, locked up the lab, and walked the forest trail down from the cliff-top to his home. It was dinnertime. He always took special care making sure he broke from work and visited with his parents over the evening meal.

His dream, coupled with staggering inspirational flashes, had become his master. He felt it important not to lose touch with things most important things in life: one being quality time spent with the ones he loved.

Walking out from the trail into the opening near the house, he noticed a car in the portico that he didn't recognize. Being slightly put off by unannounced visitors, he shrugged, put on his social hat, and went in the back door, which led to the kitchen. Savory scents wafted through the air; his stomach growled.

"Enricco, is that you?"

"Yes, Mom," he said, stopping and sitting on the bench inside the door to take off his work boots.

"We have a little surprise for you!" his mom said, smiling.

Probably an aunt and uncle stopping by to show off their new car, he thought. Putting on his happy face, he entered the kitchen. There she was. Older, a little curvier, hair longer—and that smile. "Oh! My goodness! Monique!"

They rushed to meet halfway. He picked her up in a big hug and spread a dozen kisses on her face and neck.

"So you're happy to see me?" she asked.

"Happy? Hell, I'm overjoyed; it's been years."

"Well, yes, but only two."

"Only two, she says. Mom, can you believe her? Leaving me here alone to go off and explore the Universe with her mountaintop telescope, naming new planets and stars, while I sweat and toil in my workshop, attempting to build the ship that will one day take us there."

Setting her down and placing her arm's length away, he said, "Let me get a good look at you…. Wow! You have grown up! You look, well, I'll not attempt to put your gorgeousness into words, but I am short of breath, and my heart is pounding! I think it's just dawning on me how much I've missed you!"

Taking her face between his palms, he kissed her on the lips, longer than the peck of friendship and pressing a bit harder into her softness, breathing in her fragrance. "Thanks for coming," he said, upon breaking the kiss. "Moni, it means the world to me. How long are you here for?"

His mother got one of those Mom-knows-all looks. She sighed and smiled dreamily, as though she could already see grandchildren running rampant through the house.

"I've taken a position. I left the observatory in Touraine and have accepted a long term contract here," Monique said.

"Here, as in the U.S.?"

"Here, as in University of Berkley." Monique examined him closely. She knew him well. She was prospecting for his true feelings. She watched him intently, attempting to weigh his reaction.

"Berkley...? Our Berkley? Here across the bay from San Francisco?"

"The very one!"

In those eyes, she saw the minutest flicker that spoke his heart, while he said, "That's fantastic! Will they be working you ragged like your government has been, or will you have days off to come and play here in the mountains with me, as we did when we were children?"

"The contract is for a set one hundred sixty hours a month. I have complete flexibility with my hours, so I can easily take some three-day weekends, if you'll have me."

"Have you? Careful, Moni, you're giving me ideas, ones I shouldn't be talking about in front of my mother."

"Well, I have to go to the study and roust your father for dinner," his mother said. "He's becoming a bit forgetful. I'll get out of your hair. Just relax and talk about anything you want. Rest assured, I won't be listening, and if I do happen to hear anything juicy, I won't tell. I promise." Beaming, she left the room.

The two old friends looked at each other, without speaking. The bond between them, sealed so many years ago, pounded in their ears. No words were necessary. In the ensuing silence, their eyes spoke volumes.

FOURTEEN

Cobran and Sabrina watched from the leased mountain house. Monique and Duhcat were playing like children, running trails, watching sunsets, and enjoying their reunion with excited exuberance. The two were inseparable on Monique's days off.

The plan had not been completely laid out for Monique. Her contract had stipulations in the fine print that spoke of necessary information gathering, yet the clause was vague. Covered in legal language was the catch. It was cloaked using terms one would presume spoke of scientific research, yet which could also be construed as covert intelligence siphoning.

Monique was living in a beautiful historic building. Her condo had bay windows overlooking the city and the coastline as well as the Golden Gate Bridge. She had bought a new Mercedes 500SL convertible coupe. All aspects of her life had changed drastically since accepting the position and contract. Cobran decided it was time to set the hook, but Sabrina thought it better to let her settle in for a while longer before dropping the bomb: that they expected her to spy upon Duhcat from inside his lines of defense. The debate began. Sabrina was coy, feeling things from a woman's perspective, while Cobran analyzed what he perceived to be the big picture.

Cobran started the conversation after a pleasant afternoon. They had eaten, swam, made love, and napped in each other's arms. No sense bringing up a stormy subject before the best part of the day was behind them, he thought.

"Sabrina, I think it time we inform Monique of her *real* agenda with Duhcat, before they get more intimately involved."

"Listen to me, dearest," she said, smiling, the setting sun illuminating the features he had grown to love and desire. She had a little smirk, as though this conversation were under her control and that no matter what he thought, she would prevail.

Cobran enjoyed her spunkiness and independent mind. His intellect rose to meet hers on occasions like these. They made a great team, he thought, as she began the presentation he knew she had gone over a hundred times in her mind.

"A woman desires security; it's a primal instinct with us. We have offered her a great package, yet she has lived it only a few months. She needs to raise her comfort zone, to live the life we've granted her without restraint. Monique needs to fall into *needing* the lifestyle, to take the lure of being able to purchase anything she wants; *that*, to a woman, is crucial, and we've given it to her. It's too early to drop the bomb, as you are so fond of calling it. This is all so new to her that her loyalty to Duhcat will prevail. What is your rush anyway? Aren't we having the time of our lives?" She stroked his chest lightly, nuzzling his ear, kissing his cheek while she wrapped herself around him. She could feel him weakening.

"Sabrina, the general is constantly asking for progress reports. Frankly, the contract we signed with Monique made the old man's eyebrows raise higher than I've ever seen. He asked if the woman was even necessary. I assured him she was, and he assured me that we had better see some results quickly, for the expense invested." He sighed. "There's more."

"Spill it all, darling. I want to know you're deepest concerns…your innermost feelings, doubts, and trepidations. Tell me. I am, as always, your ever-helpful sounding board."

"You are such a little smartass! It's a good thing you're so cute. And you *are* ever so helpful." He fondled a breast, as if to punctuate his sentence. "Otherwise I would think you're being sarcastic as hell."

"Me?" She feigned innocence.

"Yes, you."

"Go on, dear, I'm all ears." She batted her sleepy, bedroom eyes.

"I'm fearful that when the two of them become physically intimate, she will never betray him. Instead, Monique will tell him all about our designs and foil the carefully laid groundwork upon which we've worked so hard the past two years."

"Darling, a woman scorned. Do you remember the beginning of that old saying?"

"Hell hath no fury. Where are you going with this? Can you give me a clue?"

"If Duhcat were unfaithful after they became intimate, she would betray him in a heartbeat."

"What makes you think he would be unfaithful? She's pretty damn hot! If I weren't with you, I'd be the wolf-howling at the full moon in *her* back yard."

"Oh really? You find her that compelling?"

"Oh, it's probably just all those stories you hear about the sensuality, intelligence, and romanticism of the French culture—not her staggering looks *or* her fabulous body." Cobran smiled, letting Sabrina know unmistakably that he was teasing and attempting to get her goat.

"The romantic mystery of the French culture has your intellect in throes, not your incessant libido?"

"Definitely my intellect, nothing remotely resembling libido."

"You are such a little liar! You *do* have a thing for her, don't you?"

"No honestly I don't, it's all business between her and me. All business, I assure you, dear Sabrina. You hold my heart in your heavenly clutches; no one else."

"My clutches…. That's really romantic, Cobran. Can't you think of something better than that?"

"I'll try. I promise. Can you give me some time? I'll come up with something that will really knock your socks off!"

"You had better! I'm still fuming, knowing that all this time you have been doing more than just watching her professionally."

"You are fuming? I love it when you fume."

Cobran grabbed Sabrina, pulling her close and kissing her neck. "Could you hold that fume until our discussion is over? I really feel we should move this thing forward. Why would she feel scorned if Duhcat were not unfaithful?"

"Because, sweetheart, we will deviously and ingeniously construct some evidence from thin air, which does not even have to be true but that shows him in a compromising situation with another woman…a *gorgeous* one. Then Monique is clay in our hands. She will do anything to make him suffer for the betrayal."

"You are a wicked-thinking little wench. I'm so glad I chose you for this partnership."

Pulling Sabrina close again, he whispered softly into her ear, "Are you still fuming?"

"A little. Could you fan the embers for me?"

FIFTEEN

Duhcat and Monique had been spending every weekend together. The common bonds and old friendship were picked up like they hadn't spent over two years without seeing one another. They both worked extra hours during the week, and Monique took three-day weekends.

Summer was grand. The mountains boasted rushing rivers of sparkling water. Evergreen forests rustling in warm afternoon air scented the breezes with the spicy flavors of cedar fir and pine. Wildflowers bloomed across the vast alpine meadows in an ever-changing kaleidoscope of vibrant colors.

One sunny afternoon, they sat along a little creek listening to the rush of birds sweeping past, singing, each possessing a signature call. They both felt, without speaking, that they could be in no more perfect place. They often sat comfortably without talking. Other times the joy of conversation ran between them, a natural current flowing effortlessly. Today, however, Moni had been quieter than usual.

Duhcat sensed she wanted to talk of something important but didn't really know how to ask or where to begin. "Why so quiet, dearest?"

"Ricci, am I really dearest to you?"

"Moni, if you only knew how I feel about you, your question wouldn't be necessary."

"Why don't you tell me? I can't think of anything I'd like to hear more."

"I'm not sure words would suffice, precious. I could scratch a pen on paper for weeks, only to tear up each weak effort. Words strain under the breadth of the wonderfulness of you. But I shall attempt the impossible, if you insist."

"Oh! I absolutely *do* insist!"

"My feelings for you are as vast as the evening sky. I see the aurora borealis and it strikes my eyes and heart with mysterious beauty, yet it is a weak flicker when placed beside your stunning features. The alpine wildflowers paint a picture striking to the heart, yet they pale when you sit framed among them. The river's voice has always spoken to my heart, but when I place its cherished sounds beside the rush of your breath, I would happily give up all the rivers of Earth, if I were forced to choose between the river and your breath beside me. Sunshine warms my body with its golden-fingered touch, yet you warm my soul with a glance.

"The days we've spent together recently...I frame in my mind each scene, each of your smiles, the sway of your hips, and the sunlight casting colors through your hair. Oh Moni...if mere words could suffice in describing the multitudes of joy I feel each time I hear your car coming up the mountain, we would need a thousand days for me to speak without pause."

"You take my breath away, Ricci." She moved a little closer, and he to her. They wrapped their arms and legs together as they lay beneath an azure sky. They moved, as they had never before, together. The rush of winged flight stilled and the breeze abated, as though Nature herself longed to observe their passion.

SIXTEEN

Monday morning came, and Monique was more than tired. She was elated at the same time. Finally, after more than a decade of desire, her dreams had been fulfilled. They had spent a weekend together that was far and away beyond her dreams.

All those past years of longing, all the desires they had forcefully kept in check...all that passion had been let loose: a tsunami of emotion and relief, of bonding, and of dreams, both of the past, at last lived, and those of the future.

They had always loved one another, from the first time they had met...now they were one. They had melded in the most ultimate sense. They had worn one another out.

Monique checked the floor-length mirror after dressing for work, making sure she was not as bowlegged as she felt. She smiled, thinking of the past two days with him. A tingle of butterflies flitting in her tummy rose, crested, and then, after some time, subsided. The butterflies rose again anytime her thoughts drifted to those intimate hours spent in his arms.

She turned and looked in the mirror, straightening a few strands of her strawberry blonde hair. Something was different about the way her face looked. She stilled her reverie for a moment and looked deeply into the mirror, analyzing what she saw. She giggled, concluding humorously that the only explanation was that she *absolutely* glowed.

Grabbing her small purse from the foyer table, she walked to the elevator and pressed the basement button. The little stainless steel box whisked her twenty stories downward in a second or two, and she walked out of the sliding doors and to her sleek little 500SL.

The engine caught on the first flick of the key, and she thought, as she cleared the cool shade of the garage and broke into a glorious day boasting blue, that life could be no more perfect.

Ten minutes later, she was on campus and through the security gates for government-only personnel.

Walking into her office and closing the door, she wanted to be alone and to collect her thoughts. She drifted back to the weekend, closing her eyes in heavenly reverie. A knock came at the door. Startled, she called out, "Yes?"

"It's Sabrina.... May I come in?"

Monique rose reluctantly, resenting slightly the intrusion into her wonderful daydream. She opened the door, and Sabrina entered, flowing in behind the door's swing as though she were attached and operating on the same hinges. "Cobran needs to see you right away, in his office. Five minutes." The intruder looked Monique over, taking special notice of the flush on her cheeks. "Feeling all right? You look a bit flushed."

"I'm fine. I probably drank more coffee than I should have this morning." In actuality, she rarely drank coffee, and hadn't had any that morning.

"Don't be long. Cobran will be reporting to the general as soon as the three of us finish the meeting." Sabrina flowed out the open door.

Monique heard the swish of her skirt as Sabrina walked briskly away, down the corridor. Monday morning could have started a bit slower, she thought.

Monique picked up a notepad and her small business valise and made her way to Cobran's office. She tapped lightly on his door, which was ajar.

Cobran moved quickly towards the opening, spreading the door wide in a gracious flourish. His demeanor was warm; his eyes were intense. Sabrina watched coolly, in silence.

"Monique! Great to see you! Been a while since we've had a chance to sit down and talk. Please." He motioned to an open chair and, after she entered, closed the office door behind her.

"How was your weekend?"

Monique felt his prying eyes searching her face for something, but for what, she could not be sure. "Wonderful, thank you for asking. And yours?"

"Oh, work, work, work! You know me…don't ever get much time to just slow down and watch the river run by. How are you getting along here? Do you enjoy your position?"

"Actually, yes. I want to thank you for the opportunity. I was so bored in France, so stifled. Here I feel the sky is the limit!"

Sabrina and Cobran shared a slight conspiratorial glance.

He began: "Monique…the general has requested something special of you. The impetus for the request comes from much higher up the chain of command. It has to do with planetary security and is of the utmost importance. Do you understand?"

"Not entirely, sir."

"Oh Monique, you can dispense with the sir. Just use my name when addressing me. We are all friends here, aren't we, Sabrina?"

"Of course!"

"Just call me Cobran, will you?"

"If you prefer."

Monique's antennae were up. These two seemed a bit nervous, and there should be no reason for such a feeling; they had always been pleasant to her, yet today their actions seemed forced. It was as if they were masking a hidden agenda, as if they were attempting to smooth out her defenses. She couldn't really place her finger on why she was uneasy, only that she was.

"Cobran, what is it you wanted to see me about?"

He glanced furtively towards Sabrina again and cleared his throat. Monique noticed tiny bits of perspiration beginning to show on his forehead and temples, even though the room was cool.

He cleared his throat again. "I...*we* need you to do some undercover work, for the government. The project is cloaked in secrecy, so anything spoken of here today cannot be repeated. Do you understand?"

"Yes. Of course."

"We need you to gather some important information on your long-time friend, Enricco Duhcat." Cobran paused and waited for her response.

"What kind of information are you after?"

Cobran leaned forward to whisper, lending his words greater importance. "We need to know when his ship will be nearing completion."

"Why don't you just ask him? Why do you need me? I was hired here for technical astral physics, not to be a spy or secret agent. You must be joking! Tell me you are! You are, aren't you?"

Sabrina stepped in and took control of the conversation. Cobran seemed to be at a loss for words.

"Dear, really, it's not spying—only sharing information. Surely you understand that planetary security is of the utmost importance. We only want to keep our world safe. That's all. It is really very simple."

"Why me? Why not someone trained to be a spy? Why would you ask this of me?"

Cobran said, "We are not asking. This comes as a direct order. You are being ordered to accomplish the task, not being asked."

The bomb had been dropped. The room became silent.

Monique's mind reeled. "I was hired as a researcher, not as a spy…I can't."

It was Sabrina's turn. "Hon, don't be alarmed. Your contract is implicit. It states that you are to complete *all* research to the best of your ability, as required by the director. This bit of research is necessary and is required by the director. It is really quite simple."

"And if I don't play along?"

"You break your contract, your 250K per year evaporates, along with your car and your visa. Don't make us play that game. We like you, and you are doing a wonderful job here. We want you to fulfill your contract and stay the duration."

"So you're threatening me?"

"*Threat* is too harsh a word. *Enlighten* would be more appropriate." Sabrina tossed a manila envelope on the desk in front of Monique. "Here, you might want to take a look at these."

She opened the packet and gasped. There were photos—many photos—of her Ricci in the arms of a statuesque blonde. Monique looked intently at the photos and immediately knew this was no game. If she didn't play along, she would be back in France in a heartbeat. After quitting her job at the observatory, she would be ranked lower. She would find it hard to get something that even paid the pittance she had been earning before she left.

"Okay," she said.

"Okay what?" Cobran asked.

"Okay, I'll do it."

"Good choice! You'll see. It will be a piece of cake. But you have to be discreet. No use having Duhcat onto the game. Can you do that?"

"Of course, discretion is my middle name. Can I keep one of these photos?"

Cobran shot a look to Sabrina, attempting to see her reaction and allowing her the latitude to step in.

"Sure, hon," said Sabrina. "Don't take it too hard. He has a lot more women than just that one chasing after him."

"Can I go now?" asked Monique.

"Sure. Just keep us up to date. You visit him nearly every weekend, don't you?" Cobran's voice was steady, but Monique saw his eyes flitting back and forth between Sabrina and her.

"Yes."

"Good. Good. Then make us a weekly progress report, and I will pass it along to the general. We need to keep him satisfied. Without his political support, our funding could be jerked in a flash, and none of us want that, do we?"

"No. Of course not. May I leave now?"

"Absolutely! Thanks for your help! Who knows, with the right information, you may be receiving some very substantial bonuses!"

Cobran smiled, and Monique saw the false sincerity. It was like a line drive, smashing into her face.

"I'll see you two later."

SEVENTEEN

Duhcat listened intently to the conversation between Cobran the information gatherer, Cobran's cute little sidekick Sabrina, and Monique. He had known for months this play would happen. The inflection in Monique's voice gave away nothing but her irritation. He could not be certain whether she was just playing along or simply pretending too, but when he saw her in person, he would know in an instant.

Monique, and his love for her, was an irreplaceable jewel; this he knew.

His love of the stars was a power that had been born into him. It held him. It was a certain magnetic attraction so forceful it drew his soul nearer...towards the great black beyond and his destiny. Every day of work on the ship brought him closer to being within the expanse of vastness as yet untraveled by humans from Earth. He would choose between the two—between Monique and his dreams—without hesitation if necessary. He prayed it would not come to that.

Throwing himself into his work, he quickly relegated the problem to a compartment at the back of his ever-working mind. The weekend would be here soon enough, he thought, and she would be in his arms once more.

The ship secreted beneath the surface was nearly finished. *False Trails* was also mostly complete, or as complete as the decoy would ever be. It only needed to misdirect the ones who were plotting to steal his intellectual and personal property for a short time. Duhcat had thought the quandary though like a master of chess: every possible move and countermove had been plotted and accounted for. Soon the game would begin in earnest.

As Monique strode back to her office, her blood boiled. Her temperament as a red head was solid but easily cast into a flutter of emotion. She breathed deeply, calming herself, pondering the dilemma, searching for the solution. She knew there was a doorway that would lead her out of the predicament; there always was. She just had to find it.

What raised her temper was the obvious: they had hired her to get at Duhcat. The offer had been too good to believe, and yet here she had been only a few moments ago, thinking that life could be no better. *How could he?* she thought. Could the photo be old? But even then, they had always had something special…or was it just *her* feeling that way? None of the tormenting questions could be answered without *him*.… Then the hammer dropped: she must spy on her beloved or be sent back to France in disgrace.

Monique's sharp mind raced ahead, and a plan formed. She could not speak with Enricco. Anything outside of their normal course of communication would be observed and noted, and she could be put in extreme jeopardy. Anyone with half a brain understood the lengths to which the government would go in the name of planetary security. Casualties were commonplace. She resolved not to be one of them.

On Friday, she would go to him. Until then, she would do her job diligently. She would keep a good face on for everyone here at the research facility while she silently wove an invisible fabric of a plan that would support her future steps, however dangerous they might be.

After Monique left Cobran's office, Sabrina had closed the door quietly and looked to him. She desired to hear his thoughts before imparting her own.

"She didn't look too happy about her new duties," Cobran said, and then stopped talking. He was threading the verbal trail without giving too much away.

"No, she was obviously not happy with our bomb."

"What do you think, Sabrina?"

"I think I would like to hear what my darling boss has to say about the short little meeting we just concluded. Shall I make notes?"

Cobran smiled. Sabrina had placed one leg forward and turned slightly sideways, so that he could take in her form. She was teasing him. Her words were professional; her posture was enticing.

"I really don't know. You women are so complicated. Just when I think I have the feminine gender figured out, something assaults my mind, and I feel like I'm sitting in my sandbox playing with my toys, understanding nothing of the great wide world. I feel sometimes as though my knowledge of the opposite sex is no more developed than when I was a young boy."

Sabrina laughed. "Poor little Cobran! I bet you were a really cute little boy, and the apple of your mother's eye. You'll have to show me pictures sometime. I'm sure that with that mischievous smile, you could get her to do most anything for you.... But I'm not your mother."

Sabrina fell silent once more, hoping the void of conversation would prompt him.

"I think our wonder boy has gotten to her. That's what I think! This guy is so abnormal! He has fantastic looks, is in superb physical condition, has arguably the most brilliant intellect of our time, and he's the heartthrob of nearly all young women who have been near him. Hell, you can hear the syrup dripping from their correspondences with him. Why would she be any different?"

Sabrina looked thoughtful, and then said, "We are paying her a fortune. She has the car of her dreams, a condo to die for... I guarantee you, right now she is, like all women who are placed in a similar predicament, adding up the value of her contract and its many gratuitous perks and then placing all that on the scales. She will then place our 'wonder boy,' as you so affectionately refer to him, on the other side of the scales. The heaviest package wins. Simplistic, streamlined, ruthless, and, above all else, true to a woman's primeval survival instincts. The photos were a nice touch. Did you see the look on her face when she opened the packet? That's what I think. Now you spill!"

"Sabrina...I had no idea. I had always thought that we men were the ruthless ones, easily detached from feelings of the heart when something of greater substance was offered in replacement. Now you want me to believe it is actually the feminine gender that possesses that streak of determination; that cold, hard, brutal, and emotionless power of evaluation that leaves Shakespeare's thoughts and formulas of love in the lurch?"

"You are off point purposely, Cobran. You are attempting to evade your obligation to spill your true thoughts. I am waiting. We can discuss the philosophical merits and differences of the genders another time. Right now, let us stay on point." Sabrina fell silent, knowing the first one to speak would be in the weaker position.

"You are good! In many ways.... Okay you win. Our girl is torn. I believe she is, as you say, weighing her options, and their values. She loves it here. I have eavesdropped on her casual conversations: she feels like she has landed in paradise, and she now has the man of her dreams, and a career to die for...tough choices indeed. I think she will play along with us, at least for the time being.

"Only the future will tell if we are correct. Let's pray that we are.... Sabrina...is that what you've been doing with me? Weighing me upon the scales against your position, your perks? If something extraordinarily better presented itself, would you be so calculating, so ruthless? Would you leave me in the lurch for it, and not look back?"

Cobran looked intently at Sabrina. A vulnerable spot within him lay exposed as he fell silent, waiting for her response.

"You are a good boss," Sabrina said. "You have many other talents I enjoy as well. If I were to tell you all my thoughts, desires, and dreams, I would lose all my mystery and my intrigue. I would become bland, and soon your roving eye would find another more appealing, or at least one who possessed the illusion of something more appealing. I prefer to keep you guessing. Hopefully, you will not forget this conversation and always place your best foot forward. If ever you start failing in that... it will mean the beginning of the end for our personal relationship." She looked at him and let silence punctuate her statement.

Cobran thought her eyes literally smoldered. One of her curved hips was cocked out, and she had one hand resting on her waist on the opposite side. She stood otherwise erect, and he could easily see the rise and fall of her breath. Her scent had become so familiar, every time she was near he felt his heart increase its pace.

Sabrina smiled wide, breaking the serious moment. She felt empowered, seeing him falter for words while he took in what she had said. Then she became all business, saying, "We place her under full security screen. I want to know if she burps in her sleep. If she attempts to warn him, we must know. We have monitored their digital communications, their flow, content, and symmetry; the slightest change in their communications will mean she is trying to warn him."

"My, my, you *have* been thinking about this."

Sabrina sidled up to him, exaggerating the sway of her hips. Cobran's eyes moved back and forth with them. She smiled to herself, thinking, *A few more steps and he would surely be hypnotized.* "We women are not *just* the softness men seek. We are the subdued and hidden masters of the men who become addicted to our passionate wiles." She nuzzled his neck as she pressed tightly to him. "Are you my willing servant, Cobran?"

"Your wish is my command. Lead me; I am yours!" Cobran chuckled at his attempted humor. Within her embrace, his mind ran the question, *Is she joking?*

EIGHTEEN

He sat upon the edge of Blue Bend's massive granite face, his legs dangling in thin air. Work had worn him out. He was waiting...waiting and resting. His arms and legs ached, and his mind wandered in fatigue. It wandered in and out of the game being played. Monique would be here soon, and he felt anxious, which was a foreign feeling to him. He thought about the game and wondered what side she would play on. He chuckled to himself. Monique was a dream come true; he hoped she would not become his nightmare as well.

Far to the west in the valley below, he saw the flash of sunshine off the windshield of her car. Soon the smooth whine of its power plant could be heard, and then the inevitable shifting of gears, coming up the winding mountain road. She was driving a bit faster than her usual Monte Carlo style, he thought. She obviously had something on her mind, something that was creating her rush to get there.

Duhcat walked casually towards the house. He wanted to greet her when she arrived. He needed to gaze deep into her eyes and interpret the language spoken there.

The silver 500SL coasted gracefully to a stop in the drive. He stood in the shadow of a pillar, watching her movements. She wasted no time fussing with her hair as she sometimes did; she simply threw the door open and strode towards the entrance.

He stepped out of the shadows as she neared, and she started slightly in surprise.

"Moni, darling, you look heavenly!"

He grasped her and spun her in a circle, taking in the wide eyes and the flush on her face. She began to speak, and he planted his lips on hers, kissing the words away. As he softened the press, he said, in a whisper so light, she could barely discern his meaning, "Not a word."

Her eyes acknowledged the message, and they walked hand in hand towards the house.

Entering the foyer, he said, "Mom, your favorite girl is here!"

His mother came bustling from the kitchen, saying, "I thought you'd never come! You are later than usual, dear. Oh! You look over-heated; your face is so flushed. Are you feeling well?"

"Better now that I'm here. It was so hot in the city, so smothering." She looked at Duhcat, wondering whether his feelings for her were true…or just a game. "But the mountains are wonderfully cool at this altitude. I'm really fine. Please don't worry about me."

"Let her go and freshen up, Ricci. A woman needs a few moments to herself after being on the road for hours."

"Of course. You know the way, Moni. I'll be in the kitchen, giving Mom a hand with dinner."

He watched her as she strode across the living room and disappeared down the hall.

His mother noticed the wistful look on his face. "When are you going to ask that gorgeous creature to marry you, Ricci? Your father and I aren't getting any younger. It would sure be nice to have some little ones running about the place…don't you think?"

"Mom, I do think a lot, but I don't always share all of my thoughts with you. Is that all you ever think about? Marriage and grandkids? What if I get the ship ready and then Moni and I decide to jump in and have our children on another planet?" He smiled disarmingly.

"Oh, you are such a tease! You wouldn't dare…! Would you?"

"If you keep pressuring us, I just might."

"Oh! Oh my! Have I been? I haven't meant to…it's just…you know how I love children…."

"Yes, Mother, I do."

Monique came into the kitchen.

"See there, doesn't she look much better? Not so flushed. Cooler, aren't you, my dear?"

"Yes, a splash on the face did wonders."

"You kids run along and relax. I don't need Ricci here supervising my efforts. Go and visit. I'll call you when the meal is nearly ready."

They each chimed in "thanks" and walked out the back door and into the woods.

They walked for a while in silence until they were well into the forest. Duhcat took a small pad of paper and a pencil from his pocket and handed it to Monique. On the first page of the tablet was written, *"Don't speak of your troubles. Write them down."*

She took the pad and scribbled, *"They want me to spy on you!"*

He took it back, and wrote, *"I know. I knew before they hired you."*

"And you never told me?"

"I wanted to see what you would do."

Monique grabbed the notepad. *"You were testing me? After all these years? After how we've always felt? You wondered if I would betray you? I guess we need to start over, because you don't even know me!"*

Monique threw the pad and pencil in his lap. Duhcat noticed that along with the pad was a photograph he had never seen before. It was a picture of a gorgeously statuesque and stunningly beautiful blonde sitting in his lap without a stitch of clothing on. In the picture, the blonde and he appeared to be looking deeply at one another.

Monique stood up and began walking away. He jumped up and caught her before she had taken a step. He wrapped her in his arms. She stopped, because he would not let loose.

She struggled and would not look him in the eyes.

"Don't you see, Moni? The fault in the photo?" He spoke so softly; it was barely a whisper.

"What fault?" she whispered back, still not looking into his eyes.

"Look at it. Do I ever look at you that way? Tell me what's missing. Tell me why this clever forgery makes no sense!"

Monique took the picture in hand and studied it for a moment, and Duhcat saw the light flash in her eyes. She stopped struggling and melted in his arms. "I never saw it before! You look like you're solving a math problem. You never look at me so cooly."

Duhcat whispered softly in her ear, "Exactly. Don't you see they are trying to separate us so you will work for them? I have *always* known you, from the moment we met as children. We have known each other's hearts. I just can't take the slightest chance with this project. That's why I never told you what I knew: that they hired you to get on the inside. Monique…the ship, it *is* me. It is my life. Please forgive me."

Falling softly to the forest floor, they said no more.

Lying out of breath beneath the ancient pine trees, they watched the limbs pushed by the breeze rake back and forth in a sea of motion. A variety of winged life flitted through the forest, calling songs that serenaded their refreshed hearts. As the sun crept lower in the sky, and its light changed from the brilliance of the earlier day, the colors changed and melded. The platinum light became golden yellow streaked through with violet and dark grey. Undulating cumulous clouds were moving in from the ocean and beginning to cross the coastal range.

"Feels like rain coming, Moni. Did you bring some warmer clothes?"

"To be honest, I didn't. I so wanted to see you, I rushed in packing."

"Not a problem; I have some Paul Bunyan loggers shirts and some cork boots. I think you'll look pretty cute in suspenders and a felt hat."

"Maybe I'll choose to wear nothing but you all weekend. Think you could handle that?"

"Sure I could, but I'm afraid one side of you would always be cold."

"Well, when I get cold on one side or the other, you'll just have to change sides, won't you?"

"Whatever you fancy, darling."

"Really, you are being so easy, so soft and pliable. I feel you are clay in my hands just waiting to be formed into something very special."

"I'm already something very special. Haven't you noticed?"

"Oh! I've noticed. Maybe you should cover that up before your mom comes to find us for dinner!" Monique began laughing, and he followed suit, their voices echoed back from across the valley, joy ringing its ancient healing bell.

"We better get inside," he said, "before they think the wild animals have dragged us off."

"Well, I do feel like I've been devoured by a ravenous beast. Have I satiated your hunger?"

"Only temporarily. I think you would make a delicious after dinner dessert as well."

"You! You never stop. I love the way you always turn the direction of our conversations subtly towards sex."

"Sometimes not so subtly, and it is called lovemaking here in the U.S. Haven't you had that language lesson?"

"No. Perhaps you could teach me the finer points after dinner."

"I would be honored."

Enricco rose and offered his hand. They dressed quickly, and he began laughing as he watched her.

"What is it?" she asked.

"Here…you have a pine cone stuck in your hair!"

"Oh my! I'm an absolute wreck! Your mom is going to think I'm the epitome of the brazen French hussy."

"Aren't you?" he said, laughing and pulling her close. "Ever since I was a young boy, I have loved no other than this very brazen, very French, and just slightly hussy woman. You grasp and hold my attention. If you were anything less…would I long for you as much?"

"Ricci, can we sneak in the back way over the roof and into your bedroom so I can change without your mother seeing me carrying half the forest floor on my clothes? These pine needles and mosses just won't let go."

"Sure. It has been nearly a decade since we snuck in or out."

They stepped lightly, sneaking up towards the house, using the shadows of the trees. They could see his mother working in the light of the kitchen, and they snickered at the absurdity of them, both in their twenties, skulking in the shadows like a couple of juvenile delinquents.

They climbed up the arbor along the wall of the garage and then walked the roof to Enricco's room. After sliding the window open, he handed her in and then climbed in behind her.

"Ricci, could you go to my car and bring me my bag? You'd better change first. You have half the forest clinging to your back as well. It looks like you've been doing summersaults. Was I that frantic and rough with you?"

"Tough love, babe. That's what I like."

They both broke out in suppressed giggles, attempting to choke them back so they would remain unnoticed upstairs. He changed quickly and was about to step out of the bedroom door when she stopped him by grabbing ahold of his shirt. Reaching into his hair, she pulled out half a pinecone. "You might want to leave this behind," she whispered.

"I'll cherish it forever. Until we meet again." With a bow and a flourish, he was gone.

Monique sat on the bed and waited. Her mind rolled in splendor, and her head lolled in relaxed circles while she contemplated the evening. She thought, *He is so right for me: sexy... well, much more than just your average; the ultimate in handsome; charming; funny; and not wrapped up in himself or the least bit conceited. How and why have we been magnetized to each other all these years? I'm so happy I could cry!*

The door opened, and he crept in like a burglar, tiptoeing up to her and handing her the bag in a conspiratorial fashion that made her giggle quietly some more.

She changed quickly and was ready just as his mother called out the back door that the food was nearly ready. They crept down the front stairs and went quietly out the door, and then walked around the house and answered her call.

NINETEEN

Sabrina and Cobran sat on the terrace, gazing across the valley at the granite cliffs, which were showing the setting sun's play of colors and shadows. They both wore a miniature earpiece and were listening to Monique and Duhcat. After the pair went into the house for dinner, they broke from duty and went inside as well. The evening had turned chilly after the heat of the late summer's day.

"Gee, those two seem to be having all the fun!" Sabrina said. "Such dedication to our work. Do you think you'll have any energy left for me, after we fix our evening meal?"

"Does that mean we are done for the night?"

"You should know their routine by now: dinner, a bit of visiting with the parents, and then they run upstairs like children and jump in the sack with the music on. Dish doesn't pick up anything understandable in those circumstances, so we might as well call it and get up early. He won't be working tomorrow, so perhaps when they go hiking, as they almost always do, we can eavesdrop then."

"Okay, boss!" Cobran had begun calling her that affectionately because she had a good mind for strategy, and he didn't at all mind empowering her and following her lead.

Changing the subject to food, he said, "How about we take a quick shower and then run to that cute out of the way Italian place."

"I haven't done anything physical; I don't really need a shower."

Cobran gave her a suggestive look that made Sabrina lift one eyebrow.

She smirked. "So you are saying I *will* need a shower?"

He nodded, and then he swept her up in his arms and carried her into the master suite.

TWENTY

Duhcat woke as the first traces of the rising sun cast pale light on the walls of his bedroom. Monique lay quietly beside him, her red-blonde hair fanned onto her pillow, framing a face he had adored since first seeing it over a decade before.

He trusted her. She loved him and had come of her own accord. She had told him about the meeting earlier in the week with Cobran and Sabrina.

However, allowing Monique to know everything—all of his plans and when he would be ready to depart aboard his ship, *Intrepid*—would only place her in jeopardy. Running the game through the gauntlet of his mind produced the same answer, no matter the data he entered into the quandary.

He could not risk giving her the whole picture. The necessity of the situation, which would shortly come to brinkmanship, could not be weighted on her or placed in her knowledge. They could drug and induce her to talk; she might never even know she had given up strategic information. And so, in pondering and searching for the proper path, Duhcat had decided.

She stirred beside him, and he took up one of her hands. The fingers twitched lightly as her eyes opened. She searched the room briefly—the ceiling, the walls—

as though not sure where she was, and then those wide-set, gorgeous, blue-green eyes landed on his. She smiled wide.

"Morning, love," he said.

"Hi, baby." She rolled into him and squeezed. "I was dreaming I was back in France, at the observatory, and that something had happened—something that drove me away from you. I was so miserable, I wanted to jump. Then I woke, and you're here, with me. Ricci…everything will be all right…won't it?"

"Absolutely, my sweetest charm," he said. "Worry not. Your warrior is here to protect and save you from the demons and dragons that haunt your sleep. Rest assured, I will make sure you are safe, in your waking hours as well."

He smiled disarmingly.

When he smiled, the darkness in his eyes lifted slightly. If a person were fortunate enough to witness the phenomenon of his genuine smile, it was like seeing into an angel's eyes: something pure, uncompromising, wise, and tender all in the same breath. Monique thought all this in silence and then said, "Love you," as her mind ran through the same thoughts it had contemplated countless time over the years when attempting to understand what force within the vast universe had chosen to create him…to make him *so* special.

"I am *hopelessly* under your spell," Ricci said. "You are the electricity that makes my clock tick, the moon that runs the tides of my emotions, the rain that waters the vast desert of my love when, after a time without your company, it becomes so thirsty and dusty it could be blown away by the winds of a life that loses tender beauty without your presence."

"Where does it come from, Ricci...the words flowing from you? The sentiments that make me melt?"

"You inspire me, darling. The nourishment I need comes from right here!"

He dove beneath the covers, kissing her tummy and other soft spots. Her mind whirled in abandon. The ceiling came in and out of focus, until she closed her eyes.

After breakfast with his parents, he asked Monique, "Would you like to see my shop? I swear, I will do no work. I am all yours this weekend and every weekend you come here. But I've never shown you my project... and I would like you to see it."

"If you think it wise..."

"It's all fine. Let's go."

Enricco's mother lifted her brows, saying, "No one has ever been in that shop, dear. As odd as our son is... this might be the closest thing to a proposal I've ever witnessed from him. Sometimes I begin to think he's married to that ship he's building."

She laughed at her own joke, and his father joined in.

Enricco stood gracefully, comically taking on the air and overly pompous mannerisms of an aristocrat, and said, "Come, darling, let us leave these catcalls behind and journey into the great beyond, together. Mother, Father, if you will be so kind and excuse us?"

"By all means, son." His father's words were accompanied by a look of humorous adoration.

As they walked out of the dining room, Monique could hear his mom giggling and saying, "Oh, isn't she *so* wonderful?"

"Yes, I do believe Ricci has his hands full this time. I have never seen him look at any young woman the way he does, Monique."

"And what about the way she looks at him? The adoration...it *literally* oozes. Think of the beautiful grandchildren those two will have! Oh, I'm so excited...I can hardly sleep!"

"Yes dear, I know you are fond of her; she has always been an exemplary young woman. She has made away with a piece of my heart as well."

They went out the back door once again and into the woods. Walking deep into the tall pines, Enricco stopped and handed Monique a note. She read in earnest: "*All that you see today, all that I tell you, may be repeated to them. Please understand, I have thought this entire game through and have decided this is the best path in dealing with their desire for information. This is all I can say to you. Do you understand?*"

She nodded her head, and he took the pad back and slipped it the back pocket of his well-worn jeans.

Walking out of the trees, which brushed and rubbed with the morning's sturdy breeze, they came out onto the flat of the cliff's top. They walked across to a modest building where Duhcat placed a hand over a small screen. "This is a scanner. It checks bone DNA, fingerprints, and blood type; it's almost impossible to fool."

The door opened, and then closed automatically after they walked into the unlit shop. Overhead lighting flicked on.

"These lights are full spectrum. They give off a near perfect simulation of the sun's light, making it a lot easier for me to work long hours without my eyes feeling strained. Come."

He took her hand, and they walked through a small room with computers and a control panel that looked quite complicated. The next door opened into a large warehouse-like space. In the center rested something that made her heart leap.

"Ricci, she's so beautiful. Her lines create the illusion that she is weightless, already in flight. Why does the prow turn downward? It's the mirror image of graceful ships I have seen in history books. And why does her skin shimmer and pulse, as if she is a live organism?"

"She is. Her shell is neither metal nor composite. You see the strands of DNA in the animals and plant life, which decomposed millions of years ago and became crude oil, were integral to those living organisms feeding off of mother Earth and her minerals. Modern man has made steel and various alloys from the metallic ores, and plastics and composites from crude oil…but no one before has bred the two."

"Bred?"

"Yes! You see, both materials in their many variations are intrinsically related, having elemental makeups that came from Earth's molten beginnings: the rich minerals and metallic particles originally from Earth's body. Why not mate the elements that have existed in symbiosis since Earth's beginning?

"By this inspired concept, I have been able to grow an organism that is not metal nor alloy, and not a composite of plastic.… You see, each of these components have weaknesses within their molecular structures. Alloy is strong but in most instances brittle; composite plastic, more lightweight, more pliable, but not as durable; and then we have to consider effects such as corrosion, radar bounce, electrical grounding issues, and magnetic interference, which could affect the ship's drive system, weightlessness, and gravity."

Duhcat picked up Monique and spun a circle playfully. Setting her down, he continued.

"Her skin is a living organism. It heals itself and is multilayered, pliable, durable, and non-magnetic. It resists friction, much like our skin. The energy from impacts is absorbed as the impacting mass is bounced away. "Think of rainfall: it fills the rivers and lakes; the dams hold the water, storing its energy; and then once it's released, its energy is converted into electricity. Her skin does all this and more by absorbing the energy, and redirecting it to the propulsion mechanism. It is very complicated; I don't expect you to understand. I am just beginning to understand it myself. To me, this whole project has opened my eyes to what can be, what should be, and what will be in the near future.

"Moni, many of the designs implemented in her construction and drive systems were inspired flashes that came to me after much study and reflection, sometimes even in my dreams while I was sleeping. Actually, I ask for answers. I ask whatever you would like to call it, the Cosmos, God, the Infinite intelligence of the universe. I can't explain all the whys. I just know that the answers I've received come not from me, but from somewhere out in the vastness of Deep Space."

"Ricci, what is to become of *us*...when you board her? When will you come back?"

"I don't think I *will* be coming back... There is nothing here to hold me but my parents and you. My mother and father are growing old. They wish for me to pursue the dream...the thing I was born to find. It's out *there*, Moni, not here.

"Earth, when I think of her, brings great sadness to my heart. She is being rapidly destroyed, and there is nothing we can do to stop the destruction in time. I believe Earth is being pushed to the brink and will continue a steady decline. I don't want to be here, to see what she will become, to see her indescribable beauty defaced, to see what was once pristine laced by the filth of greed. I can't have those pictures in my memory. I desire to remember her as she is now: still staggeringly beautiful in so many places. Please don't allow me to start in on that subject. We are here, looking into what *can* be the future, not the past and what *should* have been.

"Moni, I am hoping you will come with me…come and fly the stars with me: be my co-pilot, my wife…"

"Just tell me when. I will have some goodbyes to say," she said. "But is it truly possible? We are taught that the sheer distance even just to the center of our galaxy would take many lifetimes to travel— Wait. Was that a *proposal?*"

"The people of Earth were told that the world was flat, the speed of sound was an impossibility to break, Mount Everest could never be scaled by man, and the four-minute mile was out of the question. Visionaries with inspired dreams proved all those beliefs to be false! My quest is the same, only it is happening within our lifetimes. It is not some marvel breakthrough we read about in the history books; we can live it! And yes," he said, smiling, "that was."

"A proposal?"

"Yes."

"What kind of proposal? For me to be your partner in life, in justice, and in crime, if necessary?"

"Crime is a relative term. In one culture, an act considered a crime would be commonplace and completely acceptable in another. Yes, to your question; I want to leave Earth, with you strapped into the seat beside me. We will see things that no one from our world has seen. Only in my dreams have I witnessed the places we will visit.

"There is one place in particular: a garden by the sea, where there are massive stone columns just as in ancient Greece. There is a waterfall that sings; the melody can be changed by simply moving the stones upon which the water falls. There are fountains and arbors full of grapes, and blue-green mountains with peaks covered in the white of fresh snowfall. I have seen us there together. Out there lies my destiny…a destiny I want to share with you. It will be an adventure of discovery, of rebirth."

"When, Ricci?"

"Soon. I have to finish the drive systems, but the shell of the ship is complete. Then we must provision her for the trip. I'm not sure exactly when we can leave…less than a year, I think."

"What shall I tell them?"

"All that I have told you. Understand, I am giving you *only* information for them to receive, nothing else."

"But what if they are listening now?"

"They can't. The same skin that protects the ship protects my shop, and it is soundproof. We are safe speaking here. But you can repeat all that I've told you. Trust me, darling."

"I do."

TWENTY-ONE

Cobran sat with Sabrina across the valley from Duhcat's workshop. When Duhcat and Monique entered, the listening devices quit picking up. The soundproofing and filters effectively cut off all vibration from within the confines of Duhcat's work area. They took out their earpieces and looked at one another. Sabrina was beaming.

"What has you so fired up? I can see your gears spinning. Give!" Cobran exclaimed.

"She's in! You know no one has entered before. She's working her magic, getting him to trust her. Don't you see how important this is? We now have eyes and ears inside. We are no longer blind. Soon we will have a sketch of the ship!"

"A lot of good a sketch will do us when we have little else."

"You can be so pessimistic at times. Why don't you look at the bright side? We are definitely making progress! Don't you think?"

"She is inside. You can surely call that progress. But don't you ever get the feeling that he's just toying with us? That he's giving up only the information he wants us to have, and nothing else? That he knows we're hacking into his computers and listening to their conversations, and that we've only hired her to get inside? Has anything I've just mentioned crossed your mind?" Cobran looked to Sabrina in the silence that followed.

His question pounded in her mind. "Actually, no. Why would it?" she asked, perplexed.

"Because, we are dealing, for all intents and purposes, with a master of chess; he's obviously thought the game through, plotted the possible moves, and made provisions to sacrifice necessary pieces to block our main thrust, all the while wearing down our momentum. Could that be the case?"

"Boss, darling, it could be, yet I rather doubt it. He's so engrossed in his project, and with her. It seems to be all-consuming. I don't believe for a moment that he would waste a lot of time on strategy or on allowing us to hack non-strategic info."

"Is that what you really think?"

"Yes, truly. Do you believe differently?"

"In fleeting moments, certain doubts *do* cross my mind. I guess it is only when a chilling uneasiness comes over me. Just think: tracing a hack job is not that complicated, and we have dozens of staffers who do just that all day and night. How could we deign to think Duhcat hasn't traced our entries? And if he has...wouldn't he take precautions?"

"He has! He changes his encryptions like underwear. He's obviously being extremely careful. But he is only one man. He would have to spend every hour of every day to protect himself against the resources we have running twenty-four/seven. Relax. You are worrying yourself over something we have little control over. In the end, we will have what we want. All his hard won inspiration, intellectual property, and the designs for the ship. I assure you!"

"I'm not trying to be a wet blanket here.... I just think we should be realistic. This Duhcat, he strikes me as a telepath. Have you researched the work the Prodigy Section has been accumulating on the subject?"

Sabrina shook her head.

"Well, you should. It will open your eyes to a whole new world of possibilities."

"I will place it at the top of my list!" Sabrina smiled, taking in Cobran's mood. She had never seen him like this and wondered if what he had said had some merit.

"When they come out of the shop, we should get a feeling of whether he is playing us." We've fed all of their previous conversations into the computer and programmed it to search for minute discrepancies."

"I guess," Cobran began, as his brow furrowed deeply, "...I guess I just hope we can come away from this project shining like the brilliant stars that we are. You know what happens to the masters of projects that end up stinking, don't you?"

Sabrina said nothing. She only shot back a concerned look, which bridged the silence. She was attempting to keep Cobran talking on track.

We would be cast back to the bottom of the heap, only it would be different then. We would have a big black mark that would not be erased for the rest of our careers here. Our chance to rise through the ranks would be endlessly stifled. You see how important success is?

"If Duhcat manages to make fools of us, we might as well forget our plush government pension and re-enter the private sector where our secret record would not follow."

"Sweet one, I will work extra hours, do my due diligence, and study the ins and outs of telepathy. I will do all that you ask to keep your fears from becoming reality. Does that make you feel better?"

"With you on my side, I always feel better!"

Sabrina smiled warmly and then stood. She walked over behind him and began rubbing his shoulders. "You are so tense! Just relax. Let me take all that worry and stress away."

As Sabrina massaged, her mind ran back through their conversation. She felt the niggling of doubt as well. *Could Duhcat just be toying with us?*

TWENTY-TWO

Enricco Duhcat had awakened before sunrise, as usual. His work was nearing completion, and every day he arose excited about the final preparations. As he finished dressing to go down for breakfast, he heard rapid footsteps coming down the hall. They belonged to his mother.

"Ricci! Come quick. Something is wrong with your father."

Duhcat sprang for his bedroom door, opening it in the same motion. "What is wrong, Mom? Where is Dad?"

"In our bedroom. I found him using the plunger in the bathroom sink, and I asked if it were clogged. He looked at me with a strange, distant look and said, 'Of course! You know those damn snakes!' And then he went back to frantically plunging the sink drain. Oh Ricci, I'm so worried. I've never seen him like this!"

They rushed to his parent's bedroom and found his father still engrossed in his work.

"Dad...are you all right?" Enricco asked.

"Of course! But I have had it with these damn snakes; I'm showing them no mercy! That's all! They are always slithering up the pipes, breeding in them, obstructing the flow. I'm going to kill each and every one of them!"

"Mom, go and get a flashlight! I'll back up Dad."

His mother rushed away, leaving the two of them alone.

"Dad, snakes don't like bright light in their eyes. Mom's getting a flashlight. I'll shine it down the drain. That should send the buggers scurrying!"

"Good idea, son. I'll keep them at bay until the reinforcements arrive!"

"Good thinking! Here she comes now!"

Flashlight in hand, Enricco slipped up beside his father, clicked the light on, and gave the old man a conspiratorial look. "I'm in position! Shall I let them have it?"

"Give it to them, son! Sear their stinking butts!"

Duhcat slammed the flashlight over the drain as his father jerked the plunger clear.

"Take that, you slippery vermin!" Duhcat shouted.

A moment later, his father said, "That was a great idea! I was getting weary of plunging, but I wasn't about to give up!"

"Thanks, Dad! You've saved us again!"

He hugged his father lovingly. His mother looked on from behind, concern and bewilderment etched into her normally serene face.

"You must have worked up an appetite. Let's get some grub!"

"Sounds good, son. Let's go!"

Later in the morning, Duhcat was helping his mother tidy up the breakfast dishes. She had been quiet, obviously mulling over the morning's excitement.

"Mom, I know you are concerned, but the doctor said this type of behavior is to be expected as Dad declines. You know he loves us and would do *anything* to protect us. That's all he was doing. Please, don't fret. It breaks my heart when I see anguish in your eyes." Hugging her tight, he said, "Love you, Mom. I love you."

"I'm so happy you are here, Ricci…I don't know what I will do when you leave!"

She began to tear up, and Duhcat said, "There, there now…everything will be fine. Don't fret."

Marina Duhcat looked up into her son's dark eyes. The golden flecks sparkled.

"I can't help it sometimes, Ricci. It is a mother's place to worry a bit now and then."

She smiled as well, and the two of them looked into each other's eyes—eyes that were so familiar, they granted comfort to each other, from their lingering concerns.

TWENTY-THREE

Duhcat knew they would come soon. The intense hacking into his systems had minimized drastically in the past few days, and he felt the raid would be any day.

He had not wanted to set his mom to worrying about things beyond her control, so he had put off speaking with her about the matter until the last minute. Now it was time to warn her. There was no other possible way.

He walked down the hill through the giant lodgepole pines that separated his cliff-top workshop from the house farther down the hill.

Entering the back door, he sat down to take off his work boots. His mother's ever-caring voice asked, "Is that you, Ricci?"

"Yes."

She walked into the back hall from the kitchen with a concerned look on her face.

"Was something wrong with your lunch?"

"No, Mother. As always, the lunch you sent me was wonderful."

"Oh! Good. I was worried. It is so unlike you to come home at mid-day."

"Mom, we need to speak together about some things: important matters that cannot go on un-discussed."

"Well, dear, you know I am all ears. Is this about... about you and Monique? Oh! Do tell me you've asked her! Have you?"

"Well, that wasn't really the topic I wanted to talk about...but since you are so curious ..." Duhcat let suspense build for a nano.

"Oh! You bad boy! Keeping your dear and doting mother in suspense! You know my blood pressure. Ricci...?"

"Yes, yes, Mom. Monique and I...we will be getting married. We have yet to set a date."

Marina Duhcat began to dance. It was an ancient Italian tradition. It was the dance of joy for her. Duhcat could see mist in her eyes, and the most beautiful smile he had seen on her face in years...a smile he had not seen since he was a little boy.

Her feet flew, and she grabbed his hands, drawing him into the fun. Soon she was out of breath and stopped to embrace her son.

"Oh, I have been waiting patiently... haven't I, Ricci?"

He laughed at her happiness. "Yes, Mother, you have been the example of patience," he lied.

"I can see them now!" she said.

"See who, Mother?"

"The grandchildren: all those little ones running about the house, of course! Oh! This is so wonderful...I must run and give the news to your father!"

"Mom! Wait a second. There are some other things that won't wait. We must speak quietly of them first. Okay?"

"Yes? What things, Ricci?"

"Mother, soon we are going to have some visitors... not the friendly kind. Government people who want some things I have been working on. Please do not be alarmed. Everything will work out just fine. I just need you to promise me to keep an extra close eye on Dad for the next few days…until they come and go. Can you do this?"

"Of course. Are you sure everything is okay, Ricci?"

"Yes. I have been expecting them all along, but now… the time is at hand. On another note…it's about the grandkids running about the house. The ship is ready. I want you and Dad to come with Monique and me. You will have to enjoy children while we travel the stars…. You know my dream better than anyone. I used to sit in your lap as a small boy and share it with you, on evenings when the sky was black velvet and the countless celestial bodies spoke their voices to me."

"Grandchildren on a space ship?"

"Yes, Mother. It is the *only* way." Duhcat looked at his mother in a way with which she was intimately familiar. His look told her that he had set his mind. She accepted it, and agreed instantly.

"Oh! Oh…alright! I don't *really* care where we are, as long as there are dear little children of yours and Monique's running about! Besides, this big old house is just too much trouble for your father and me to keep up anymore. I could get used to a tidy little space to live in!"

"You will soon see that the space is none too small, Mom."

"Can I go and tell your father the news about you and Monique?"

Duhcat looked to his mother, taking great pleasure in the joy etched into her face. She seemed, in that moment of ultimate happiness, to have grown much younger. Hugging her for a moment, he said fondly, "Yes, Mom. Go and tell Dad."

TWENTY-FOUR

The President and his advisors sat in a meeting requested by the Joint Chiefs of Staff. A few of the uniformed personnel within the room visibly bristled as they pondered the topic of the meeting. Future technology that would affect the intensely competitive branches of planetary armed forces would be determined in the meeting.

The President's mind wandered as the overbearing brass jockeyed for position and power within the group. His advisors looked distant. A few others looked close to dozing, bored with the repetitive arguments emanating from the armed forces' top echelons. The meeting's subject matter was a young man who had been under intense surveillance for nearly five years: Enricco Duhcat. All involved in the meeting were speaking of *taking* Duhcat's intellectual property; they used words such as "seize" and referred to Duhcat as a "planetary security threat." One of them pointed out the public displeasure with the trillions of credits worth of funding that had been circling the drain for decades, going into the proverbial black abyss of "governmental research" with no tangible advances.

It appeared that those in the meeting would justify the past and future funding by seizing Duhcat's intellectual property and telling the public that this was the fruit that had finally ripened from a government tree that had been cripplingly expensive to grow.

Planetary government had constantly reached deeper into the pockets of the vanishing middleclass, gobbling up the little extra for which the diligent had been striving. Little was left for the masses at the end of a work year except for them to be more frugal, stretch a credit, and make do with a promising dream turned sour. There was no escape from the treadmill that slowly burned the fuel of billions of lives.

The monopolizing industrialists, bankers, and government, bent on growing a stronger stranglehold on the common people of earth, had formed a mold cast in concrete and impregnated with the steel reinforcing bars of laws that protected the vast wealth of a few and gobbled the lives of a slaving generation. The next generation born would be indoctrinated with visions of a grand dream that was only an illusion. The new generation arising would be consumed and burned in the same brutal manner as the last.

The president took in the meeting with an air of nonchalance. His quick mind was focused on the upcoming election and how he could turn the events being spoken of in the room to his electoral advantage. At no time did he think of Duhcat as a person, nor weigh in his mind the disastrous path being spoken of in the room, a path that would soon sculpt future history.

His personal cell phone rang. He looked at the incoming number and immediately stood.

"Gentlemen!" he said, in a voice of which any president's wife would be proud.

The room quieted from the previous discontent.

"I have an important personal call. I beg all of you to excuse me for a few moments."

All heads in the room nodded assent, although they actually felt dutiful resignation that the President was leaving the room and would not be available to witness the staunch debate that had ensued and was nowhere near finished.

Walking out and closing the door, the President answered graciously, as if he were speaking to a loved one. "I'm so honored you called; it has been ages!"

The voice on the other end of the line was raspy and unemotional; it sounded like a voice that had been weaned from tender youth on harsh Cuban cigars. "Jack… how's the family?"

"Good, good, and yours?" The President had never met the caller's family but felt sure that he must have one…somewhere.

"All fine." The voice was curt, signaling that introductory graciousness would be replaced by business. "I understand you are in the middle of a very important meeting."

The President paused. The meeting was under the tightest security screen and was only known to a very select group. "Carl…you never cease to amaze me with your uncanny knowledge of inner-government workings."

"I'm surprised I still amaze you. How in the hell do you think my family and their vast interests have become the most financially powerful on Earth if we weren't always in tune with the many varied and often fanciful notions of global politics?"

The line went silent as the President tried unsuccessfully to think up a response.

He replied, "Well, it is indeed a great pleasure speaking with you."

"Yes…I am sure it must be! Now, about the campaign: you *are* intending to run, aren't you, Jack?"

"Yes! Yes, absolutely! I will, of course, expect your ongoing support. I can count on you, right, Carl?"

"Well…" The caller let the silence go on painfully.

Finally, the President caved. "Perhaps we have a bad connection…. I can count on your ongoing support, Carl, can't I?"

The caller ignored the question and said, "The connection seems very clear on my end. The topic of the meeting you were pulled from, Mr. President, was interesting. I would enjoy hearing your take on the subtleties."

"What interest would you have in this meeting?"

"Enricco Duhcat and his work is…shall I say, drawing to me, and to my interests. Perhaps you could share with me the temperature of the contest. I understand all the armed forces are vying for position, literally drooling for the bounty Duhcat has so naively allowed us to intercept."

"With all due respect, Carl, I can't share anything from the meeting with you! All within its confines are top secret."

"Listen, Jack…I know about the meeting. I know the topics. I know of Duhcat and his test scores. I expect you to give! Share with Papa!"

"I can't! It would be a breach of my oath and of my office!"

"Jack…have you even taken the time to analyze and understand the massive amounts that my companies and our spheres of influence have donated to your previously beleaguered and—as some had called it—anemic bid for the presidency?"

"Well...actually, no. The grueling contest was all that consumed me. Of course I appreciate your support and always have. Surely you know that!"

"No, Jack, I don't know! My...our sphere of influence accounted for 64.69% of your campaign funding. Do you mean to tell me you never took the time to connect all the dots?"

"I'm a very busy man, Carl."

"As am I! And I have taken time from MY family to attempt to make YOU understand how strategically important the support we have *lent* you is. Are you beginning to understand, Jack?"

"I am trying to...64 percent did you say?"

"No, I said 64.69 percent."

"Oh...yes, 64.69...that's right."

The President faltered, and the silence once again became a most provocative and disrupting force. Beads of sweat appeared on the President's forehead. He had not experienced such nervous sweating since directing his first trial many, many years before.

"So, Carl..." he asked, "where do you and I stand?"

"The jury is out, Jack. I can't say. Do you want to talk as old friends?" The voice was not friendly but it alluded to a friendship rekindled—or one that could be rekindled if the proper responses were offered.

"Yes! Of course! Yes. Let's talk as old friends."

"Good! I am satisfied that you see the intelligence in listening very carefully to what I am about to impart. Otherwise..." Carl let the silence work again. "...Otherwise, my sphere of influence is looking at Delgato for 2016."

"What?" The President was incredulous.

"It's a great name. It means skinny in Spanish. The Hispanic populous of registered voters is soaring. They will all vote for him, leaving you and your community far behind!"

"What is it you want, Carl?"

"I want Duhcat's work seized. It cannot be left to the common man, as Duhcat dreams. We must stop him at all costs! Do you realize that if Deep Space jumps *were* possible, all the best and the brightest would migrate? The intellectual seed that gives Earth its edge would no longer be under our control. Do you understand?

"We have a barrier. For all intents and purposes, the people of Earth, the little people, the underprivileged, are trapped here. They have no choice but to be happy with the scraps we allow to fall from our tables.

"Am I getting through to you? We would be left with the worst. Earth's gene pool would rapidly decline. Anyone intelligent enough to understand what we have been forcing down their throats for the past two centuries would leave…if they were allowed to. And that is exactly what Duhcat has planned. Don't you see, if we lose the intellectually creative, if the best and brightest are allowed to migrate—Earth would be cast into a rapidly spiraling descent…a death spiral. It will not do."

The President's sharp mind was in shock. He was attempting to grasp the words just spoken, but the ideas were abstract and completely out of his normal realm of thought.

"I'm all ears, Carl." He mustered this response to show his willingness to consider what was being imparted without actually committing to anything in particular.

"This Duhcat is no different from the many extraordinary intellects who were also visionaries in our past," Carl continued. "We must treat him no differently. His work must be seized and withheld from the public. I don't care *how* it is done, Jack…I just want your assurance that it *will* be done!"

The President stammered out an answer that was a forgone conclusion. He had sold his soul to the special interest groups that lobbied, spending their vast pools of credits to support those who would do their bidding. The long road these groups had travelled was littered with the careers and bodies of those who had refused them and not made pacts with the Devil; now they were washed up political has-beens…or worse.

"Of course, Carl. You have my word. It will be done."

"Jack, I always knew you were an intelligent man. Keep taking those smart pills, and we will get along fine. Good day."

The line clicked and went dead.

The President dropped into a chair, pondering the revelation that was just beginning to sink in: he had joined the ranks of the soiled. He had had such high hopes and aspirations, before being elected. Now, darkness closed in and shuttered his once honorable soul away.

TWENTY-FIVE

The special-ops team wore black. They had sworn allegiance upon donning the uniform. Their loyalty was not to the common man, nor to their brothers and sisters of Earth. They were company men, born, bred, and indoctrinated since youth. Their master was planetary government. It was the mother that had birthed them, and the family they had sworn their lives to protect.

Five charcoal-black gunships thundered towards Blue Bend's sheer face. The crescendo of the game was about to unfold. Each aircraft held ten men who wore hardened battle armor and bullet-proof helmets, complete with mirrored face shields; the scene was something from a black dream: surreal and ominous to behold.

The men thought of the target as a highly fortified and dangerous position, one they had been ordered to take and hold, but if they had known it was an undefended family's home and workshop, it would have made no difference. The orders were clear. They would be followed unerringly.

Duhcat locked the door to his workshop and walked towards the beginning of a trail that led into the tall pines. He would have looked odd to anyone watching because he was wearing full raingear, with a hood and rubber boots, yet the day was bright and sunny. There were no clouds in the sky.

He had no desire to be near when the edgy automatons of planetary government arrived. He intended to let them have what they came for without the least bit of struggle or potential for confrontation.

The trail slipped down the side of a sheer canyon where a waterfall dropped its wet spray through sunlit air. The cascading sheet, in free-fall, glistened in the golden rays.

As Duhcat hiked deeper into the cleft, he heard the faint throbbing pulsations of multiple distant rotors pounding air. The sound grew louder until he could feel the reverberations in the ground.

Duhcat walked to the pool at the bottom of the falls, skirting the water's edge, and neared the cascade. The wet, drifting spray began coating him. He stepped behind the falling water and into a small concave depression in the granite. It wasn't really a cave, but the space afforded him enough room to be out of the water and comfortably out of sight. His presence would be undetectable by infrared scanners.

He prepared to wait until they had what they came for. He would wait until they were gone.

He heard the sound of the aircraft throbbing above the pitch of the falls. Soon the ships quieted and the ground ceased vibrating. *They have landed,* he thought. *A few hours and it will all be over.*

TWENTY-SIX

Anton Duhcat had been dreaming. He awoke from a familiar and nightmarish scene. The dream had come for years, but, he mused, recently its frequency had increased. The dream took place in his youth, when he, as a drafted soldier, had become the lean, mean fighting machine Viet Nam demanded. The jungle had devoured all the others: the soft, the unwise, the arrogant, the ones who displayed unintelligent valor, and the ones who slept too soundly. The steaming jungle... so green, and yet, he thought back, on many days it bled red with the blood of his brothers in arms.

The VC were near. He could feel the unmistakable tension in his muscles and the rushing prickles running through his skin. The hair on the back of his neck rose. *Warning!* the signs were saying. Signs that he as a hunter, one who had been hunted countless times, knew as a true old friend.

Charlie is coming! he thought.

Anton rolled out of bed and crawled to the closet, where he kept his guns. Donning his old uniform, he slipped out of the bedroom window silently, carrying a backpack full of ammo and his vintage M-16.

He could hear the rumbling sound of distant helicopters. The heavenly hughies, they had called them in Nam, he remembered. The salvation any bush soldier longed to hear when their fat was near the fryer. Reinforcements were on the way! It was a wondrous sound.

Using trees for cover, he worked his way nearer to the cliff. Cautiously placing his footfalls without sound, he stole to a vantage point where he could see out over the valley below.

The incoming aircraft were a strange black color, not the welcome combat green of friendlies. Anton rolled behind a tree and waited in the shadows.

Marina Duhcat went to check on her napping husband. She was ever so concerned about his deteriorating mental state so she had been keeping a close watch over the man she loved.

She opened their bedroom door, and gasped. The bed was empty and the window was open. "Oh my god!" she cried out loud and ran for the front door as fast as her legs could carry her.

Stepping outside, she called his name: "Anton!" But her frantic voice was drowned out by the thunder of the big black helicopters rushing in from nowhere. They suddenly appeared over the property, hovering.

"Anton!" she screamed at the top of her lungs.

Anton Duhcat could see, hear, and feel only the airships and their thunderous vibration. The tees swayed in the rushing wind created by their huge rotors beating the air.

Suddenly, lines were cast from the hovering craft and many strange intruders slid down the lines and onto the ground. The enemy was nothing he had seen before. They were dressed all in black and had full-coverage helmets with mirrored face shields. Thick, high collars rose to meet the helmets, and Anton realized at once that these strange intruders were wearing a kind of body armor he had never seen before.

Charlie is crafty, he thought. *He has a never-ending bag of tricks!*

The strange-looking invaders massed into five separate groups and moved towards his son's workshop. *Ricci!* he thought. *They are after Ricci!*

He moved from behind the giant pine tree that had been concealing him and stepped cautiously in behind the enemy. His mind raced as he pondered how he would protect his beloved son against so many.

"I've got an armed bogie on the ground, sir! Just picked him up on infrared scan!"

"Axe him, Corporal!"

The fifty-caliber Gatling gun sounded out in a short, lethal burst.

Marina Duhcat had rushed from her home just in time to see hell unleashed in the woods near her front door. She heard a sharp cry of pain and recognized the unmistakable voice of her beloved.

She rushed towards the sound, her mind a haze of screaming anxiety, and her heart racing violently. Pounding drums sounded in her ears, skyrocketing her already high blood pressure far into the redline zone.

"Anton! ANTON!"

She ran with abandon towards her dying husband.

"Second bogie, unarmed!" the corporal said to his superior.

"Let it live. If it picks up a weapon, axe it as well!"

"Yes, sir!"

Duhcat heard the unmistakable sound of a short burst of heavy machine gun fire and leapt from his secret spot behind the falls.

Something is wrong! he thought. A jagged knife of fear stabbed his heart. He had no way of knowing what had just transpired, but his sixth sense told him that the game had gone awry.

He heard the sound of an explosion, as expected. He had known they would blast his workshop door...but the machine-gun fire...

Why! his mind screamed, and he flew up the trail toward his family's home as though he had wings. The trees rushed by in a blur. Upon clearing the crest of the canyon, he heard an animalistic wail. The sound sickened his heart. The gut-wrenching wail sounded again, and Enricco knew instinctively that it was his mother, in extreme anguish.

Running towards the sound, he found them. His father was lying with his head in his mother's lap, his body torn into shreds by the sizzling bullets. She was limp and unmoving, slumped over her lifelong love, now dead.

Duhcat fell to his knees and let out a guttural scream—a release of all his broken emotions in one roaring, rumbling breath.

"Sir! Another unarmed bogie has converged with the other two, who are showing no signs of life."

"Orders stand! If it picks up a weapon, nuke it!"

"Yes, sir!"

Duhcat wept into his mother's hair and his father's seeping blood. The searing pain wrenching his heart in the spastic throes of grief only told him he had failed. He had miscalculated and lost. He had lost his family to the ones with whom he had played the game. The unfeeling machine had devoured his gentle and benevolent parents.

In that moment, Duhcat was altered. He was taken upon black wings to a place of ruthlessness and calculated cunning.

In the darkness of the dreadful space he had entered flashed freeze-frames of the near future. Duhcat saw what would happen to those responsible for the deaths of his beloved family.

TWENTY-SEVEN

The niche Duhcat had just mentally entered was observed. I Am That I Am observed Duhcat's loss. The concert of minds knew it was necessary.

I Am That I Am had chosen this man as a child, and before. His spirit had once been among them. He was a survivor. He was also incorruptible. He was one of the violent ones: the ones that had been cast afar because of the heat in their hearts, and in their minds.

The passion, the love, the cunning, and the fierceness of savage intellect that lay imbedded so deeply in him... and had never—even after eons of trying—been successfully washed away.

I Am That I Am thought, *This Duhcat feels. He experiences the savage rush of sentient beings. He is experiencing the emotions that have destroyed so many of our kind. But he has never been destroyed. He is the tool we have chosen. His future destiny has been braided into ours by some unmistakable and unexplainable force.*

He is the future. He will break away and create. He is the tool, the force, the intellect, and the vehicle that will be, for a time, bruised by necessary events; he will build a new, vibrant culture in the millenniums to come: one that will not be creatively arrested or locked away in darkness.

TWENTY-EIGHT

Duhcat did not see the trucks come. Nor did he see the helicopters sling the ship, *False Trails,* and lift it up and out of sight. Nor did he see the trucks leaving with all the electronics from his workshop on top of the cliff. These things were part of a forgone conclusion anyway.

The death of his parents was not. He could have prevented it, he thought. In the hours that had passed since the morning raid, the sun had reached its high point in the sky. At last, his tears would come no more.

He heard a voice. It spoke without feeling: "Duhcat, our orders are to escort you to a meeting. Will you come without making trouble?"

"What about my parents?"

"We have no orders regarding them. *You* must leave with us, *now.*"

The darkness in his mind spoke: *Trouble is coming... just not...quite...yet.*

Duhcat stood, his shoulders rounded. He looked at the mercenary soldiers that worked for planetary government, straightened himself, and stood erect.

The one who had spoken swept his arm towards a waiting gunship in silent instruction to move toward it. Duhcat placed one foot after another.

The aircraft lifted noisily, beating the air. As they rose into an ominous sky, Duhcat saw his parents grow smaller beneath the wind-whipped pines...until at last, he could see them no more.

TWENTY-NINE

"Mr. Duhcat, we have requested your presence here in order that important planetary security business may be concluded. We have asked you to come so that we may present a very gracious offer to you. I understand that today was very difficult for you. We are sorry about your mother and father: the unfortunate casualties of war."

"I must interrupt. What war are you speaking of?"

"The war against terrorism, of course!"

"Are you saying that you believe we—my mother, father, and me—to be engaged in terrorism?"

The general faltered. He was not used to being questioned during one of his overbearing diatribes. "I...we... in planetary government council and High Command... do not understand your intent. Nor do we appreciate the secrecy in which you have shrouded your work. Your family's vast and varied business interests have funneled all resources toward your work. Your family's vast wealth has shriveled, gobbled up by a plan—or a dream—that has never been shared. It was wrought in the utmost secrecy. What *are* we to think?"

"That my family and I are—and have always been—fine and upstanding citizens. We have contributed in many benevolent ways to Earth, her ecology, and her people. Who are you to assume otherwise?"

"Hold your questions. I am not on trial here."

"Who is then?"

The general reddened. A quickened pulse could be seen at his temples and in the middle of his forehead. Tiny beads of perspiration broke out above his brow and grew in size, threatening to become breaking, running bullets.

"I demand that you hold your tongue, Duhcat! I will not be interrogated here! I am the one asking questions! I am the one who holds your fate, which, I might add, is in a precarious balance and in my hands. We have your ship. We also have all of your computers and hidden data drives. We hold *all* the winning cards.

"Now, I know that what happened to your mother and father has made you very emotional at this time. You need to place all that behind you. You need to see that what we are about to offer you will make up for your losses."

"Are you speaking of some sort of payment for what has been taken from me? Are you saying your offer will bring my *beloved* Mom and Dad back to life?" Duhcat was livid.

"Well, now…you are an extraordinarily intelligent young man…why would you speak of absurdities? You should have invested your family's fortune in something more secure, something less controversial, something that would *not* have landed you here in front of me!"

Duhcat glared. He had never before in his life felt the emotions that were overwhelming him in this moment.

He looked to the man who had ordered the raid on his family's property as a cold-blooded murderer. *He is a murderer and nothing else!* thought Duhcat. Laws recently passed under the guise of controlling a planetary terrorist threat had made the trespass, killing, and confiscation legal.

Duhcat glared, thinking of his own laws...his own retribution, and the killing that would be done lawfully, by his own hands. He smiled: it was a forced, cool smile that had no warmth. He knew that if he didn't play the part, he would never see the light of day again. That thought forced him to be somewhat congenial...but only somewhat. He forced himself to keep cool and said, in a silky tone, "And why, General, *am* I in front of you?"

The general said, "I'm satisfied by your change of attitude. Again, we had no idea your father would attack the security team when they dropped in."

"Perhaps if you had announced your unexpected visit, my father and mother would still be alive!"

"Covert-Ops never announces their visits! Do you think we would allow you to prepare? To destroy the ship and your computers? No. No, we could have none of that. Your intellectual and personal property was seized in the interest of planetary security. Something as potentially powerful as what you have been working towards can never be left in the hands of the common man. Protecting the people of Earth is our number one agenda. Your ship, your computers, and all the technology you were about to unleash is a threat absolute. We could not risk the chance that you might destroy or release your work to the public before we could seize it."

"I am happy to release my work...the work you took. My mother and father's deaths are another matter and construe a serious error on your part: one which *will* be dealt with, in another time and place."

Enricco spoke the words calmly, seeing in his mind's eye the inevitable outcome of the game. He had failed to include his mother and father as potential casualties. The government had made a grave withdrawal: they had taken his loved ones. He swore to himself that the debit would be repaid in full.

The general continued, never grasping the maliciousness cloaked in the politely spoken words. "You will work for us. The ship can *still* be your baby, and you can run the program, with Monique constantly by your side. We are offering you a very fat contract, you being the foremost prodigy in region seven. You'll get half a million credits per year, all expenses paid, and retirement in potentially ten years…provided your ship can accomplish the vision set forth, the dreams outlined on your computers: Deep Space jumps accomplished in nanos instead of lifetimes. Do you really think it is possible?"

"Of course!" Duhcat attempted to look at the general while presenting a semblance of congeniality. The thin veil hiding his disgust and nausea must stay in place, he thought, if he were to walk free, if he were to fulfill his dreams, and if he were ever to see Monique again.

"Am I to assume that your near silence construes consent?" the general asked, taking in Duhcat's composure with seasoned eyes.

"You may, if you like."

Silence hit the great room.

"Are you finished with me?" Duhcat asked.

"You," the general blustered, in his normal overbearing manner, "Mr. Duhcat, have not accepted. Am I to understand that you are rejecting our most generous offer?"

"General…whatever your name is…I will say that your offer is a choice in front of me, and I will consider it, along with the death of my parents, and the theft of my personal and intellectual property. I'll let you know my decision before tomorrow passes. Not earlier.

"I wish to return home to tend to my parents. Will you be so kind as to excuse me?"

"Of course. The helicopter will fly you home immediately. Again, my sincere condolences." The general offered the words while his ever-active mind ran from the meeting and prospected in the future, wondering what accolades it would bring him. He spoke the words without emotion.

Duhcat saw the statement for what it was: unfeeling words formed into callous sentences, attached to a predicament that needed massaging.

"Thank you. Your kindness this day *will* be repaid, I assure you."

A cold shiver overtook the normally assured general as he looked into Duhcat's dark eyes. The golden flecks glistened, sparked by adrenalin, anger, and sheer resolve; the playing field that, until now, had been sloped greatly in favor of the opposing team, was now leveled.

Duhcat's rage was barely under control. His hands involuntarily clenched, unseen beneath the massive conference table, as in his mind's eye he visualized the general's throat in his grasp, the old eyes bulging and the blood vessels swelling beneath the sallow skin.

Duhcat wiped the picture from his mind and deftly played the diplomat so that he could walk away a free man. "General, I assure you, I will see you before the morrow is gone. Then, I feel confident, we will see eye to eye."

"Very good!" The general gloated, believing he held all the cards, and that Duhcat was mere putty in his hands. "I'm gratified to see you are considering our offer seriously. You are the missing member of the team...*our team*."

Duhcat walked from the conference hall, escorted by a security detail of five others. The room had begun to spin slightly as his vision changed from his normally grounded perspective. He walked down the corridor. The walls were out of focus. A tunnel of shifting shapes and sounds pervaded the atmosphere, but in the middle of all the negative, bustling energy that surrounded him was a small circle of clarity: within that round hole, he could see *Intrepid* and Monique. They were the only things driving him. They were all that was left of his life here on Earth.

His parents, his beloved and nurturing mother and father, were dead; it was unbelievable, he thought. *But it was true!*

A form moved from afar and into his vision's circle of clarity as Duhcat walked towards the waiting helicopter. The thing was a person, speaking to him. Duhcat, seeing it was Cobran, listened. Sabrina was by his side, a look of disbelief upon her face. Her expression matched Cobran's.

"We are *so* sorry! We had no idea where this would go...what it would come to. We offer our heartfelt thoughts and compassion to you.... Words cannot describe the way we feel about your parents' deaths and all that has happened."

Duhcat looked towards the two with eyes void of emotion and said, "I know you were not responsible for what has transpired." He then brushed quickly past them. His only thoughts were of the secret ship, and of Monique.

The center of the focused circle fell upon the waiting helicopter. It was his avenue of escape...escape from the grasp of the murderers into a world all Duhcat's own.

The rotors stroked the wind blatantly through his dark hair. The reverberations from the sound were utterly surreal to him. He strapped in, and the aircraft rose noisily into a fathomless sky. Duhcat looked briefly to the ground and saw, amongst the people below, a head full of flailing red-blonde hair. It was Sabrina's, yet it reminded him of the one he must find in all the chaos of the debacle; he must somehow find Moni. He must find her and bring her out.

The alloy bird rushed northward with its precious cargo. If any of the crew were mind readers, they would have taken note of the dark-haired stranger who sat in quiet contemplation. He was just the cargo; they needed only deliver him to the appointed drop zone and then their mission would be fulfilled. They thought of the end of their shift, and of the evening to come. In their complacency, they were completely oblivious to the events that would quickly unfold: events that would alter the course of future history. And the quiet, dark-haired man sitting amongst them was the one who would single-handedly alter it all.

THIRTY

Monique had heard nothing of the raid, the secret meeting, or the disastrous deaths of Enricco's parents. She walked toward Cobran's office with a file she needed on his desk and thought about the weekend ahead. It was Friday, and soon she would be driving north into the mountains to see Duhcat.

About to knock, she heard anxious, shrill voices emanating from the room beyond Cobran's shut door. Listening intently, she could pick out Cobran clearly. He sounded agitated.

"What in the hell was the general thinking? Does he really believe Duhcat will help us now? After his parents' deaths and the seizure of all his work?"

"Calm yourself! We must think this through clearly, and that cannot be done during the heat of anxiety and emotion! The general obviously believes that we hold all the cards...and we may yet. I agree with you: he shouldn't have ordered the raid!" Sabrina caught herself before she said something that could ruin her career.

Cobran spewed words forward without taking their repercussions into account. He was livid. His temper flared. "That arrogant old— We have worked on this for years! We were *so* close! A few more months, and we would have had *everything we needed!* There would have been no need to take Duhcat's lab by force! His mother and father would still be alive! What was the old bastard thinking? Going in like this was some sort of response to an invasion! Don't you see he has screwed this thing up royally? There is no way Duhcat is going to work with us, or for us, now! It is a blunder of epic proportions!"

"Cobran…I don't know what to say or think. The general has his advisors…and his reasons. For all we know, the orders came from much higher up, and he was just following them. We can't assume to know all that has happened in the closed-door meetings we were not privy to. You must calm down!"

Sabrina walked up behind Cobran's chair and began rubbing his shoulders, as she often did when the tension of a tight situation got to him.

He broke from her caressing hands and abruptly stood. "Did you see the look in his eyes?" Cobran had an expression on his face that Sabrina had never witnessed before. It frightened her.

"Who's eyes?"

"Duhcat's, for Christ's sake!" he blurted loudly.

"What look?"

"I'm not sure. I just know when I looked into those eyes of his, I saw something I have never seen before. There was a ruthless determination. A look that said we had failed! That we have *nothing*, and that *he* has the winning cards, *not* us!

"It was a look that made me feel like I was standing naked and alone on a frozen wasteland of ice, staring into the eyes of a very large, extremely hungry and determined polar bear: a beast that saw one thing in my presence."

"What thing?"

"Food! It was like Duhcat has already played the game to the finish. That he knows the end!"

"Cobran, stop! You aren't making any sense. It *is* terrible...what has happened, I know! But we can't change it. We must be careful. We mustn't say these sorts of things."

"What, then, are we going to do?"

"We are going to play the general's game! It's the only thing we *can* do! Don't you see?"

"No! I don't see! Nothing makes sense right now! What a freakin' mess! And we are part of it!"

"Shut up, Cobran! Someone is going to hear you! You can't talk like this! *They* won't allow it! Don't you see? Pull yourself together!"

Monique heard the unmistakable whack of a hand slapping something that sounded very much like skin. The strike reverberated through the closed door and startled her reeling senses even more.

All on the other side of the door became still. Then after a moment, the silence was punctuated by the sounds of muffled, quiet, broken sobs.

Cobran was crying.

Monique stepped softly away from his office and made her way to hers.

Entering the privacy of her office, she closed the door softly. Her mind ran on through a debilitating mental fog that clouded and nearly disabled her thinking. What was happening? she wondered. Could it be true? Had she misunderstood? Grabbing her car keys, purse, and coat, she walked briskly towards the lab.

Armed military guards stood sentry at the door; something she had never seen before.

"You can't go in there right now, miss," one of them said formally.

Glancing quickly between the two uniformed men through the small glass pane in the door, she saw a hubbub of activity. The bay doors to the cargo area were open to the outside. She could see through to the other side of the glass partition that kept the lab area sealed and clean from outdoor contaminants. Men in black military uniforms were unloading a truck full of complicated-looking electronic equipment and computers.

Alarm bells went off inside Monique's brain, yet she didn't let it show. She spun and walked down the corridor towards a stairwell that led to the parking garage below.

THIRTY-ONE

The 500 SL started on the first flick of a key. Monique drove out of the muted shade of the garage and into the brilliance of a sun-filled day. The blue sky above lent no joy to her heart. Her mind raced ahead.

When she stopped at the security gate, the guard smiled as usual and waved her through. She made way through the campus and onto the city streets, heading for the freeway. Not once did her driving give away her anxiousness and trepidation.

Once at the freeway on-ramp, Monique brutally punched the accelerator to the floor. The engine screamed through the gears. She shifted only when the valves rattled threateningly, pushing the sleek sports car to its absolute limit. She wove in and out of the late morning traffic, which was fortunately very light. The cars she passed became a rushing blur.

The green freeway signs flashed by, and she counted down the miles to the exit, not ever looking at the speedometer. After making forty miles in a bit more than twenty minutes, she realized she had been driving at nearly 120 miles per hour. Not backing off on the accelerator, she concentrated instead on the traffic ahead.

Streaking beneath an overpass, she never noticed the California Highway Patrol car tucked in behind a concrete abutment to the overpass.

The officer's radar blinked an unbelievable 127 miles per hour. He threw the radar gun into the passenger seat, swung his legs in, slammed the door, and started the engine, all in one fluid, practiced motion.

The turbo-charged mustang left two long black streaks of rubber on the concrete along with a noxious black cloud of burnt rubber as the positive-traction rear end shot the car forward.

The silver streak of a sports car had disappeared into light traffic and was far ahead and out of sight. The officer quickly reached for the radio and called for backup before his speed deemed every bit of concentration must be focused on attempting to close the gap.

Monique heard the siren first and then noticed the flashing lights in the rearview mirror. They were far behind. Cars in front of her began pulling to the side, clearing the way for the siren behind. Monique gave the little Mercedes the last bit of pedal remaining, and the speedometer ran above one thirty, although she never looked at it.

Soon, she could hear other distant sirens. She gritted her teeth, said a silent prayer that she would be allowed to make it, and gripped the wheel just a bit tighter. The screaming sirens had become a chorus of wails yet were still far behind. Her exit off the freeway was still forty miles ahead.

Another ten minutes slammed by. Her back was wet with perspiration. She slowed for an upcoming corner and glanced in the mirror. The wail of sirens had become louder. They were closing the gap.

Just around the corner, out of her sightline, lay a series of barricades set out by the Highway Patrol, along with half a dozen cars and officers. The roadblock extended to the shoulder where a steep bank rose away from the pavement.

Monique came screaming around the curve and took the roadblock in, in an instant. She slammed on the brakes, appearing to be slowing and intending to stop, but when the speedometer leveled to fifty miles per hour, she pounded the gas pedal to the floor, whipped the steering wheel to the right, and began a four-tire power-slide towards the embankment. Policemen scattered in all directions. Some dove behind their cars. As soon as her car straightened from the slide, she let off the gas, swept between two cruisers parked along side the freeway, and shot up the embankment, around the barricades. She turned to the left and headed down to the pavement on the other side.

Rocks, dirt, and dust flew, engulfing the force that was attempting to stop her. Her trusty little car banged back onto the pavement, sending up a shower of sparks that seemed like a monstrous exclamation point to many of the officers scrambling into their vehicles.

Monique didn't waste time looking in the mirror. She mashed the pedal brutally to the floor once more until the engine whined in a shrill complaint of its treatment.

A green sign announced ten miles to her exit. Then the winding mountain road would greet her, she thought, and her driving skill would be tested in the extreme.

It was then that she saw the shadow pass over her and heard the unmistakable beating sound of a helicopter. She never looked up, only focused on the road ahead.

She could see the flashing lights once more and the sound of many sirens wailed over the screaming engine.

The miles were eaten in a blur, and soon she was braking for the exit ramp. She heard another helicopter as she blew through the stop sign and took the winding road towards Duhcat.

"Ricci! Oh Ricci!" she said out loud. Monique knew in her heart if there was ever a time he needed her, it was now. She vowed she would make it to him somehow. She *had* to make it to him.

THIRTY-TWO

The helicopter bearing Duhcat back to the mountain set down upon the cliff near his shop. He jumped down, not using the ladder, and waved the pilot off. The aircraft rose, the turbulence from the rotors fanning the rising anger in his heart.

Enricco Duhcat went to where his parents lay. He carried each of them into the house and placed them upon their bed, beside one another.

He then went to the garage and grabbed two full five-gallon cans of gas. Walking back into the house, he poured a line from the front door, down the hallway and into his parent's bedroom, and then tipped both containers on their sides. The liquid ran from the containers and pooled on the wooden floor in a smooth, steady stream.

Duhcat looked to his parents and said simply, "I'm sorry."

He then went to the living room and retrieved a family photo album before grabbing some matches from the fireplace mantle. He walked to the open front door and lit the trail of gasoline. The flame caught the liquid with a whump! He left the front door open as he exited the house. The fire streaked along the gasoline trail towards his beloved parents—the family he swore, as he walked towards his shop, would be avenged.

THIRTY-THREE

Duhcat walked through the blasted and shredded door. He looked over the place he had created as a ruse. It had worked, he thought grimly, and then walked through the doorway to the warehouse area. He stopped and took in the empty room. The ship he had named *False Trails* was gone.

Placing his hand upon a certain spot on the concrete wall, he spoke one word: "*Intrepid.*"

A locking mechanism keyed to his voice clicked softly, and half the concrete floor in the big room slowly began to lower.

Duhcat slipped through the horizontal opening, and it closed behind him.

Far beneath the floor of his workshop, he walked downward through a spiraling cave, which at last opened into a large cavern. In the center of the massive chamber sat his dreams, his inspirations and his loving, sweating toil, crystalized into a form that still took his breath away. Today was one of those moments. He stood for a moment, taking in the glistening lines of the ship—*his* ship.

Then, as if he had been born for this moment, he suddenly disappeared in a tiny, star-shaped flash of platinum light.

The great cavern floor began to tremble, and all of a sudden, one sheer stone wall began to crumble and fall away. It fell down Blue Bend's cliff face and to the valley floor below.

THIRTY-FOUR

Monique pushed the car mercilessly. The tires screamed, squealing in complaint of the seemingly unending corners. *Almost there!* she thought. There were many helicopters now; the news press, along with the police, were following, filming. All she could think was *Ricci*. Her mind focused on that goal and relegated all else to unimportant background noise.

The sirens wailed behind her, but on the narrow, winding mountain road, there was little they could do but follow.

She knew the road as an old, dear friend. She could picture each winding corner ahead before she came to it. A few more turns, she thought, and then— All at once, she was sliding to a stop. The house before her was an inferno of flames shooting over a hundred feet into the air.

The forest of pines behind the house had caught fire as well.

She leapt from the car, not bothering to close the door. "*RICCI!*" she screamed.

Then, as if in answer to her call, *Intrepid* rose above the cliff edge, appearing weightless and silent in the sky. The ship kept rising higher.

"RICCI!" Monique screamed once more at the top of her lungs as she fell, weeping, to Earth, her heart feeling nothing but the anguish and agony.

He's leaving, she thought. *Leaving without me!*

The rush of sirens engulfed her senses as the cars slid to a stop all around her. Blue-clad men, catapulted from their vehicles by anger and adrenalin, drew their weapons and shouted en mass: "FREEZE."

A huge shadow engulfed all on the ground, blotting out the brilliant sun. All looked to the sky in awe as *Intrepid* dwarfed the scene below.

Monique looked up as well, taking her tear-filled eyes from the Earth where they had been focused in ultimate sorrow. She looked skyward in awe.

And then...silently, with a small, star-shaped flash of platinum light, Monique was gone. None of the officers had yet noticed. They were transfixed upon the glistening, pulsating, phantom-like ship that hovered silently in the sky above.

THIRTY-FIVE

Monique was at one moment surrounded by the police, with the ship shadowing them all from above; the next moment, she was sitting next to Duhcat. One moment she had felt nothing but trembling fear and anguish; the next, with the flick of her unbelieving eyes, she was swept away in bliss.

"Nice to see you," he said. "Quite an entourage. I never knew you were so popular!"

Monique jumped up from her seat, turned, and knelt beside him, giving him her best squeeze and a smattering of kisses. "I thought you were leaving without me!"

"I would never do that except as a last resort. But I would always come back for you. Never forget: I will always come for you. Now get back to your seat and strap in! Can't you see I'm working?"

He smiled disarmingly, and she willingly obeyed her pilot—the pilot of her dreams.

THIRTY-SIX

Back at West Coast Strategic High Command, the general was summoned urgently.

He had been napping. satisfaction had lured him to his private office, and while daydreaming of his latest accomplishments and the accolades to follow, he had fallen asleep in his favorite chair.

The intercom buzzed urgently, startling him out of the beginnings of a dream...an unsettling dream that had had something to do with Enricco Duhcat.

He answered the com: "What is it?"

"Sir! We have a situation that needs your immediate attention."

"What in hell's name is it?"

"Sir, an unidentified ship has appeared. It seems to have emerged from a massive hidden cavern on the Duhcat property. Blue Bend's face broke open, sir, and the ship is hovering above the estate."

"What the hell! What kind of ship?"

"Sir...we are not sure. It's unlike anything we have on record."

"I'll be there in a minute. Don't lose track of her, and scramble the F-28s."

"Yes, sir!"

The general trotted down the corridor, his heart pumping—not from the exertion but from the similarity between what had happened in his dream and the alert to which he was now responding.

Rushing into command central, he saw the screen filled by a haunting apparition, one that was intensely familiar: it was Duhcat's ship from his dream.

"What in the hell?"

"Sir, we can see her. She *is* visible with the naked eye, but she has absolutely no footprint on radar or ultrasound; it's like she's a hologram, sir...or a mirage."

"Mirage my ass! She looks just like Duhcat's seized ship, only a hundred times larger.

How far out are the F-28s?"

"Five minutes, sir."

"Hail on all frequencies and see if she responds."

"Sir, we have been. She is not responding. Also, sir, there is a woman by the name of Monique Delante...she was being pursued at incredibly high speeds for the past hour and a half. She screamed up to the Duhcat estate with the police right behind her—and then she vanished."

"What are all those flames in the background?"

"The Duhcat's home, sir."

That, too, had been in the dream...it was all coming back, through the fog. "Inform the ship she must respond and state her intent."

"Sir, we have been, but she remains silent. The vessel has stopped hovering and is moving, sir, albeit slowly. But she *is* under way."

"The F-28s?"

"Two minutes till they are within firing range, sir."

"Have the first group send this thing a sweet, hot kiss. You know what I mean! Heat-seeking missiles—twelve of them. I want this thing destroyed unless it responds to our hails. If it doesn't respond, let the dogs bite him in the ass."

All watched the screen as the two groups of twelve F-28 Tomcats flew at Mach 12 toward the target. Each of the twelve in the first formation launched when the group was in range.

One moment the strange ship was visible, and then, in a nano, it was gone. Left in its place were twelve small, shining discs. As the missiles neared the target site, the small discs began to streak off in different directions, and the heat-seeking missiles followed.

Soon, the twelve shining discs had arced behind the incoming F-28s and were rapidly gaining on the Tomcats from behind. The aircraft picked up the tracking discs along with the following heat-seeking missiles on radar; they immediately broke formation and began evasive maneuvers.

Shortly, there were twelve rapid explosions. The discs had attached themselves to the twelve F-28s so that the missiles tracked their own planes—until each of them made lethal contact.

"What the fuck was that?" screamed the general.

No one answered.

"Send in the other twelve. Where is the ship?"

"Sir, she has reappeared just west of San Francisco, hovering over the Pacific Ocean."

The twelve in the second formation streaked towards the new target coordinates.

"I want conventional fire on this pass! Instruct them to use only the D-U Gatling guns."

Duhcat's ship hovered in the air as the Tomcats approached, but the moment the fighters were in range, *Intrepid* was no longer there. What was left behind this time was a shimmering, glistening sheen of mist, the color of the blue-green ocean.

When the fighter jets flew through the blue-green mystery, it clung to the aircraft and began growing, covering the windows and the air intakes of the engines. It quickly engulfed all twelve.

"Sir, the twelve just disappeared from the radar."

"But we can see them!"

All watched as twelve of the most formidable fighter aircraft in the United States arsenal plummeted downward to the great blue Pacific below. There were twelve splashes, and then the room fell silent. Each and every face was stretched into varying contortions of disbelief.

"Where is the mystery ship now?" the general asked, his voice rising into a shrill whine, just short of screaming.

"Sir, it appears that she is hovering above the Moon!"

"That's impossible!"

"She is clearly visible on the screen, sir. See the shimmering dot just above the Moon's highest point?"

"Yes!"

"Well, sir, when we zoom in on that dot, here is what we get."

On screen, the image of *Intrepid* appeared.

"Call High Command into the War Room! Five minutes!"

"Sir! Many have gone home for the day. We would be hard pressed to have everyone assembled within an hour or two."

"Well get them here as soon as possible! Inform me when the other twelve are assembled." The general stormed out of command central and rushed back to his office for the file on Duhcat. The volume of material collected on the man filled two secure safes.

The general emptied the two containers into a rolling file carts. He then sat down and pondered the startling events that had just transpired. "Twenty-four F-28s!" he said to himself. "How is it possible?"

As the general entered the great room, two staff members followed with the rolling carts. A hubbub of epic proportions ensued. There were twelve around the great oval conference table, Cobran and Sabrina sat quietly on the sidelines against a wall with other staffers and aids. The general sat, fuming, and plotted his futile strategy with the other eleven members of West Coast High Command.

Finally, Cobran spoke. "Sirs, may I have the floor for a few moments please?"

The room calmed as everyone looked to the young man speaking, who was seated along the wall.

"What is it, Cobran?"

"This strategy you are considering *might* be practical *if* Duhcat and his ship were within Earth's orbit, and near enough to strike, but he is out of our reach. He is sitting up there, probably listening to everything that is being said in this room. The man is a prodigy. We should not have treated him like a common criminal. He had broken no laws prior to the raid debacle."

The general bristled. "Cobran, do *you* have a solution!"

"Yes, sir."

"Would you be so kind as to impart your thoughts?" The general's face contorted. He spat the words out with a semblance of decency; inside, he was seething.

"We return his property. We pay for all damages to him, including the death of his parents—not that money could ever replace his loss. We apologize on worldwide media for our tragic mistake. We attempt to bring him back, of his own free will. Duhcat loves Earth! I have heard him speak of her beauty countless times. We must humble ourselves and ask his forgiveness."

Murmurs rose in the room. Some wondered who the young man was, while others gasped in disgust at the proposal.

The general led the group in discussion of the merits of Cobran's comments. "First of all, gentlemen…and ladies, this Duhcat is responsible for the destruction of twenty-four—I repeat, *twenty-four*—F-28 Tomcats. He is the enemy and must be treated as such."

Unanimous approval rounded the table of twelve.

The general glared at Cobran. "Cobran, I gave you the job of babysitting Duhcat for years. No expenses were spared. You know this man better than any one of us here! How could you possibly come up with such a hare-brained scheme? You believe we should apologize and return his property, then pay a multi-billion-credit damages settlement?"

Cobran nodded. "It is the only possible solution that has even a small chance of succeeding, sir. We need him on our side; we don't need him as an enemy. You've seen what he's accomplished. Don't you worry he has other surprises in store for us?"

The general faltered, and in the ensuing silence, a technician said, "Sir, you may want to look at this."

The screen changed and showed a piece of twisted metal covered in a thin, shimmering sheen of blue-green.

"This is a piece of wreckage from one of the F-28s that crashed into the Pacific west of San Francisco. The coating *appears* to be similar to the shell of Duhcat's ship. We have recorded some tests on the material, but the one I am about to screen is our most advanced and powerful laser. This weapon can burn through four-inch-thick armor plating like a red-hot knife through butter.

Watch, if you would, what happens when we focus it at its highest output upon this piece of aluminum, coated by the veil Duhcat's ship left in front of the Tomcats, just before they disappeared from radar."

The laser beam focused on the piece of metal. Instantly, the sheen of blue-green became denser in the place of focus. The laser moved slowly in a cutting path. Behind it, in its path of travel, the burned area immediately changed and became blue-green again.

"It seems, gentlemen, that this...this organism, not only heals itself but also appears to have intelligence, or memory. It masses strength at the point of impact. Not only does it seem impervious to destruction, it also absorbs energy. After the laser's attempted burn through, the temperature of the aluminum wreckage had not increased."

"What the hell is it?"

"At this time, we have no idea. Its elemental makeup is like nothing we've ever seen. It appears to be a composite of alloy, plastics, and carbon fiber, but it doesn't have any of those components. It's as if Duhcat bred these elements together and created some kind of genetically reproducing organism that encompasses all the best characteristics."

The general spoke up. "Well, we have it, so we can study it. Surely we can find out how it is made!" He looked to the technician hopefully and received a blank stare in return.

We also have his smaller ship. It has the same skin."

"Sir," the technician said, "the material on the skin of the seized ship looks similar, but it is not the same. It's as if Duhcat left some important piece of it out. It has none of the elasticity, and none of the healing attributes, and it is easily burned through with the laser. The group would do well in watching the rest of this vid clip! If you look back to the screen, sir, you will see the mystery material no longer. Each time we attempt to study it to analyze its makeup, it simply dissolves and vanishes without a trace. It appears that Duhcat controls the organism, or the protective skin, from afar."

All eyes returned to the screen. Soon the blue-green sheen began to fade and a light shimmering mist rose from the piece of twisted aluminum. As though smoke blown away by a strong wind, it thinned and then was gone.

"What the fuck? Where did it go, for Christ's sake?"

"We haven't a clue, sir."

"What?"

"Sir, we are beginning to think the ship we seized was a decoy…"

"What the hell are you saying?" the general asked, his face a purple, throbbing mask of disbelief.

"A ruse, sir. A smoke screen. A feint."

Silence engulfed the room.

At the same time, fourteen small brilliant flashes of star-shaped platinum light lit the room. When those who remained took in the scene, they observed twelve empty seats at the great oval table, and two along the wall.

THIRTY-SEVEN

Monique, buckled into her seat, first sensed a vibration. Then she could hear it. It grew in volume. It was not frightening, as something vibrating out of balance might be. The sound was wondrous. It seemed to massage away all the accumulated stress that had been building inside her ever since her mad race to reach Ricci after hearing the news of his parents' deaths.

She looked to him in wonder, observing his hands as he deftly made adjustments to the complicated console that controlled the ship.

Then Duhcat spoke. "Do not be afraid. Equate what you are about to feel to the feeling of riding a large roller coaster, or any other exciting ride at a theme park."

Just then, she was pushed back into her seat with such force that she was absorbed by it. The seat became a sort of cocoon, swallowing her for a brief time. When the G-force lessened and she came back out of the strange cocoon, she looked to him. He was smiling wide, showing his beautiful white teeth. His eyes shone brightly as well. She loved them...but, at *that* moment, they seemed to cast brilliant piercing light into her being. She gasped at the sight and asked, "Ricci! What just happened?"

"We, my darling, have just successfully completed the first Deep Space jump accomplished by humanoids from Earth. We will celebrate shortly. However, you might wish to look out the window and gaze upon Pleiades, or, as many of us laymen call them, the Seven Sisters."

The windows of the ship suddenly opened to a picture Monique had studied from the Tourraine observatory on countless occasions.

"Oh my! Ricci…. How can this be? We are so close…I feel I could reach out and touch them."

"We are, in fact, very close. We have traveled just over forty light years away from Earth."

Monique did not speak. She looked to him, at first in disbelief, thinking this was some joke he was playing. She took in his look and realized that he was completely serious.

In that flash of understanding, it dawned on her that they truly *were* very near Pleiades. The view was as miraculous as the revelation.

"Monique, I need to check on a few items I have stowed. Would you please stay here on the bridge? If any bright red lights flash, along with an intermittent buzzer, ring me on this device. All you have to do is press this button. I should not be gone more than ten…maybe fifteen minutes."

"Yes! Of course I'll stay here and watch the bridge. My pilot has given me an order…very sweetly, I might add."

She looked at him as though she needed another kiss. Duhcat obliged graciously.

As he strode from the bridge and away from Monique, his demeanor changed. Leaving behind his love, he thought of Earth's high command and the twelve responsible for the death of his parents.

The airlock was before him. He placed a finger on the control panel and the small, airtight space was illuminated. Within the tight confines of the cell were fourteen people he had seen before.

The general pushed his way through the press of people to the window and blustered, "What is the meaning of this, Duhcat?"

"You should know, General. If you think a bit...it will all come to you...."

"What kind of hologram is this!"

"It is no hologram. I assure you."

"Then where the hell are we?"

"That, I would be happy to show you. The port window is quite small, however. You will have to take turns."

Suddenly, an oval-shaped port appeared on the far bulkhead of the chamber. It was brilliantly lit by something on the outside of the ship.

They all crowded toward it, pushing and shoving for position to see what was making the bright light.

Duhcat heard one person utter in disbelief, "Pleiades," and another said, "The Seven Sisters...but so close! So brilliantly displayed...but how?"

"That question I can answer simply," Duhcat said. "We are less than four light years away from the constellation of Pleiades."

"That is impossible!" the general said. "Pleiades is forty-four light years from earth! What game are you playing here, Duhcat! I won't be taken in by such nonsense! You are in a lot of trouble! You are being held responsible for the destruction of twenty-four F-28s and their crews. You are a war criminal. You will be tried for your crimes as soon as we are rescued, which will be happening at any moment, I am sure!"

"General...what is your name?"

"Armstrong!"

Duhcat shook his head. "No. I want to know your first name."

"William!"

"Bill…if I *was* a war criminal, I would have to be tried on Earth. As I told you before, we are forty light years from Earth. You are on *my* ship. I am the judge and executioner here. Do you remember my parents, Bill?"

"Yes! Yes, of course! That was a terrible…a tragic mistake!"

"Yes, it was. And you are the one who gave the orders. I told you we would see eye to eye before the morrow was done…and Bill, this *is* the morrow."

Duhcat dialed a control, and every one of the fourteen in the cramped chamber could hear the sound of rushing air. A nano later, they knew it was leaving, because they could not breathe. Their eyes began to bulge, as did every blood vessel and capillary in their bodies. Many could not keep their bladders from letting loose, and a few lost control of their bowels.

Within a minute, all were on their knees, convulsing, or flat on the deck, nearly passed out.

Duhcat dialed the control back up, and oxygen could be heard rushing back into the chamber. There was a rushing, gasping sound as the fourteen found they could breathe again.

The general struggled to his feet. "When I get my hands on you, Duhcat…!"

"You'll what, General?"

"I'll seek the death penalty!" You…. You…!"

"At a loss for words, General? That was a rhetorical question; you do not need to answer.

Oxygen deprivation in a partial vacuum has a way of stealing one's thoughts…and words. I know you are *very* pissed off, General. Think about how I must feel. I have not taken the lives of your loved ones, yet you have *stolen* those *I love,* from me!"

The group of fourteen must have seen something in Duhcat's eyes as he spoke of loss, because they were silenced by his look.

"Twelve of you made a decision," Duhcat said. "*That* choice is why you are *where* you are at this moment in time.... I will be brief. Aboard this ship, *Intrepid*, I condemn the twelve of you to death. By the rules of Deep Space and all that is decent. Your sentences shall be carried through at this time."

Fourteen unbelieving faces contorted into gruesome masks of denial.

Duhcat touched two controls lightly, one with each hand, simultaneously. A shimmering green-blue mist encapsulated Sabrina and Cobran, drawing them into a tight, compact cocoon. Then the airlock door slid open, and twelve of Earth's high command were sucked into the great black vacuum beyond.

Duhcat watched through the open port way as they drifted, drawn by Pleiades gravity, away from the protective envelope of his ship. Each of the twelve were speechless. If any oxygen had been left in their lungs, they would have screamed the last of their ghastly misery into the silence of Deep Space.

The airlock door slid shut, and air rushed back in, pressurizing and filling the chamber. The shimmering blue-green cocoon opened and birthed Cobran and Sabrina back into the chamber.

The two looked shocked to see that they were the only ones left in the airlock. Cobran, his voice trembling like that of a frightened child, said, "What...did you do with...the others, Duhcat?"

Ericcco pointed to the small oval port, and said nothing. Cobran and Sabrina both took turns looking out towards Pleiades. When they turned back from the sight of the twelve silhouettes drifting away from the ship, their eyes asked a thousand fearful questions. Neither of them risked saying a word. They just looked at Duhcat, attempting to understand what *he* was thinking.

He began: "I have nothing against you two personally. I understand that you were just following orders over those years of surveillance and hacking into my systems. I understand you are both appalled at the way the twelve out there, treated my parents. I have a proposition for you both. Are you willing to listen?"

Cobran and Sabrina nodded their heads frantically.

"I can see you two are in shock. The events of today have pounded my intellect with brutallity as well. I have comfortable quarters prepared for you. You will find everything you need beyond that door." As Duhcat spoke, an opening appeared behind the two. They looked towards the sound of the sliding door and back to the man who had graciously spared their lives.

"Mr. Duhcat," Sabrina began, but Duhcat interrupted politely, saying, "Please, call me Ricci. I would prefer that."

"Ricci...thank you. We are *so* sorry about your parents!"

"It would seem then that we have something in common. It is my sincere hope that we will find many more things in the days and months ahead. Please make yourselves at home. Get some rest. I will see you both again before long."

With that, Duhcat turned and walked away, leaving Sabrina and Cobran reeling.

"Did you see the general and the eleven others?" Sabrina asked.

Cobran only looked to her. He had a blank stare on his face, as though all his hope and aspirations had evaporated. He wore the face of a man weathered by dark, haunting secrets. He and Sabrina had absolutely no control over the events unfolding. They were, he thought, only puppets now. They could only wait to see which way Duhcat pulled the strings.

Cobran felt like a man sentenced to death row after all appeals had been played out. There was nothing but the counting of days until….

"Cobran! Look at me! Didn't you hear what he said?"

Cobran stared at her, eyes unseeing. The blood had drained from his face, leaving it with the pallor of someone who has already passed into the great beyond. He was, in that moment, resolving to meet the reaper, because he knew without doubt that the game he had played and the sacrifice of Duhcat's parents meant he deserved to go instantly to hell.

Sabrina, always the pragmatist, snapped her fingers before his glassy eyes, saying, "Can you hear me?"

Cobran nodded his head. His eyes were unfocused.

"Great! He offered us these quarters. Don't you think we should move out of this treacherous airlock and into a safer space?"

Cobran's glassy eyes, pulled by Sabrina's words, moved to the port light and back to the woman speaking to him.

"Yes, Sabrina…we should. But you understand that only this small opening…the one we are about to walk through…keeps us from a fate…a fate like…" Cobran looked once again toward the light. The twelve of Earth's High Command had been swallowed by the blackness of space and could be barely discerned between the brilliant light of Pleiades and the black beyond.

Cobran knew they were out there...the ones who had wronged Duhcat, and he knew *he* could be out there, too...and *Sabrina*.

"Cobran, come!" It was not a request. It was an order.

Cobran followed her in a haze of conflicting emotions. Thoughts that spoke of relativity, and beliefs ingrained during his entire life, had been swallowed—erased and engulfed by a power so forceful he could no longer think. He could only stagger blindly ahead, towards a light he could not yet see...a light he knew Duhcat held. Cobran's mind was drawn into a tunnel of light, a light he did not yet understand. It braced his senses. He knew he deserved to be out in the great black vacuum with the other twelve, but for some mysterious reason Duhcat appeared to have forgiven him. He was blinded by a brilliance seen only in his mind. Duhcat.... Duhcat, he thought, attempting to comprehend the man who had spared him and Sabrina.

He followed Sabrina, staggering towards her through the tumult, because she had said he must.

They walked through the slider, and it whisked shut behind them. What lay before them was a compact studio complete with a full bathtub.

Sabrina looked into the chilled box and found a bottle of vintage Bella Verde 1972. "Oh my God!" she said. "Do you know what this wine is worth, Cobran?"

He only looked out of his doldrums. Her voice echoed, pounding exclamation points into his brain.

"Let's drink it," he said, not actually believing that they could...thinking it was all some fantastic dream. That they would momentarily awaken with their eyes popped out, floating through Deep Space toward Pleiades, along with the despicable twelve who had formerly made up Earth's High Command.

But for some reason, a bell dinged within his enfeebled brain. It rang, admitting that they were actually not dreaming and had been spared a gruesome, miserable death. His mood brightened as he heard Sabrina uncork the bottle. Not waiting for it to air, she poured two glasses to the brim and held one up.

Handing the other to Cobran's trembling hand, she smiled and said, "To the future! And to Duhcat's proposal!"

Cobran lifted his glass weakly and brought it to trembling to his lips. "Yes! To Duhcat's proposal." But Cobran did not exude the light mood he attempted to show on the surface. His spirit was caught in the darkness of his efforts over the previous five years. The surveillance, the hacking; he was caught up in feeling responsible for the death of Duhcat's parents, and for the destruction of the family's gorgeous mountaintop home.

Duhcat walked to the bridge. He was not in the least happy or saddened. Introspection did not root into his mood. He had dispatched the twelve responsible for his parents' deaths. In Duhcat's mind, the scoreboard was even.

Entering the bridge, his mood changed. He sat down next to Sabrina in the pilot's chair.

"Everything all right, love?" she asked.

"Yes, all fine. The cargo has been taken care of."

"Where are we going now, Ricci?"

"In search of a bandage."

"A what? Monique asked, looking perplexed.

"A giant bandage of sorts. You see, Sabrina, out there lies vast and as yet undiscovered resources: minerals, precious metals, jewels, and more. Solutions Earth desperately needs are before us." Enricco swept one hand towards the spangled blackness of Deep Space, the vastness that had beckoned to him since birth. "Many of the materials are nearly depleted on Earth and are strategically important for the technological, ecologic, and physical survival of her people. Earth must survive. Perhaps, someday in the not so distant future, when the group consciousness of Earth's humanity rises to a higher level…perhaps then…she can begin to heal."

PREVIEW

A SUMMER in MUSSEL SHOALS

By: Allen Dionne

Now out in paperback and ebook formats

ONE

Boarding the Delta flight out of Seattle, I was relieved that finally, in early middle age, I was able to afford flying first class, or business class as they now call it. I avoided the security lines full of families with bickering, pimply adolescents whose iPods and Gameboys seemed sewn permanently onto their fingertips, extensions of some modern technological wave of differential idealism.

They were not unlike the silent parents who glared at one another over the tops of their iPhones and Blackberrys, thinking of the damage packing had inflicted upon their already fragile relationships.

The kids would be in that relationship space soon enough, I thought. It never failed. Except for those rare occasions that we read about but have never personally experienced. You know the kind: married at the tender age of fourteen and dying at the ripe old age of ninety-six, both within three minutes of one another, while intertwined in each other's shriveled arms.

Enough of the cynicism. I'll attempt to move through my story without more, but I can't guarantee you a thing.

For me it was long hair—the idealism, I mean. That's what set me apart from my square parents. I had, until high school, a short cut done by my mother.

She was too cheap to pay a barber for a decent job. Not that our family couldn't afford to have my hair professionally cut, I just think that she loved having me, at least once a month, under her complete and utter control.

"Grandpa is coming for a visit," she would say. No mention of my sweet, beloved and tender, cow-milking, school cafeteria-cooking, homemaker Grandma—who, since I was old enough to remember, nurtured me on her short visits with food, love, and all those understanding looks. Even if she had no idea what the seventies and long hair *really* meant, she didn't care about all that. She just loved seeing us grandkids no matter what we looked like.

Grandpa was different. Only the redneck rough and tumble logger and high climber was mentioned by my mother, as if he were a legitimate reason to butcher my hair—hair that had just begun to grow out from my mother's last foray into scissorsville.

His idea of fun was sheer torture to a young city boy: Indian wrist burns, knuckle grinds when he shook hands, the infamous knuckle scalp burn, which in modern times has been affectionately renamed the noogy. Most likely this was the least painful of his deviated and assorted shows of masculine affection, cloaked as grandfatherly love, but which I came to realize many years after he was gone were only violence subdued into something loggers, living without women in isolated camps for weeks at a time, considered affection.

Anyway, at fifteen—with the family psychologist seeing each of us children separately once a week, and then the family in group once a week—after several years of begging to grow my blonde hair long, I finally had an ally.

Her name was Virginia. An old—well…at that time anything over forty was ancient—single, chain-smoking shrink, who in my private sessions would just sit and stare at me, lighting one cigarette after another from the previous smoldering butt.

I often wondered what went through her mind in those private silent sessions. But she did say it wouldn't hurt for me to grow my hair long. Mom consented.

So in my book, Virginia was all right, if not slightly disturbing to a horny fifteen-year-old. I mean, each drag she took off her cigarette was exhaled with such a show of enjoyment, it looked to *me* like she had just finished a very satisfactory orgasm.

I never desired to get into Virginia's head or bed. I just want to thank that nicotine-stained woman for setting me free. No longer was I identified with the rednecks! I was a full-blown longhair, and reveling in my new status amongst kids my age who had shunned me before.

Hell, my hair hadn't been growing out more than three weeks when I got offered my first toke of pot. Next came the long-anticipated invitation to my first kegger.

Life was good, in a very simplistic way. That one small, hard fought and lengthily desperate battle won had catapulted me into a new and glorious life. And *that* life had brought me onto this airplane nearly thirty years later, and the story I'm beginning to share with you.

With the long hair grew an intense love of rock 'n' roll and rhythm 'n' blues. Naturally some of the Southern bands like Lynyrd Skynyrd, Alabama, and others were on my favorite playlist. Yet I had never heard of Mussel Shoals, Alabama—the town where most of that music was originally recorded—until much later in my life, long after I had cut my prized tresses.

For me, this trip was both a long deserved vacation and some well-earned quiet time to write a freelance piece I had longed to do for years. A publication called *Rolling Stone* had accepted my idea to do a history piece centered on the rise and fall of the great '60s and early '70s southern rock bands. I was their chosen author.

The title I was thinking of was something like, "The Rise and Demise of Something-or-Other..." I'm still working on that. I'm waiting for a bit of inspiration to rain down from the heavens and land in my brain.

Although, when it comes to inspired writing, I have been experiencing a three-month drought.

Believe it or not, I have not been a successful writer for very long. Good fortune hovered over me for a brief moment. I got some good reviews on a couple of novels that I had eeked out in my not-so-available spare time while working a real job sixty hours a week, and bang! I was hit in the nose with more book sales than I had dreamed of in my most optimistic moments.

Somehow or another, I had managed to hit the knuckleball of life and a home run at the same time.

Being on a constant, grueling promotional tour for nearly a year, I had become burned out. I was becoming more and more cynical by the minute. I mean, more cynical than I normally am. I was also completely out of ideas for a new novel.

Something kept niggling the back of my mind, the absurd idea that I could write a piece based on truth instead of completely make believe. I poured some mental fertilizer on the idea, and that all brings me up to this page in the story.

You see, the *idea* is to go to Mussel Shoals, to interview people who were there in the Day. I would attempt to get a different perspective on the bands, the recording studios, and how the massive wave that has long since receded affected everyday life in a little old town in northern Alabama.

TWO

The commuter plane landed. Taxying down the runway, the airport seemed so small I thought I was seeing an old war movie where the plane is forced to land at an abandoned airstrip. As we rolled up near the shabby little building that stated proudly, "Mussel Shoals International airport," I wondered at the absurdity. What famous people had this airport seen in the past? What stories could it tell? How long had it been since it had hosted an international flight?

The door of the plane opened, and a wave of humidity hit me like stepping into a hundred and ten-degree sauna for the first time. I could barely breathe. Maybe I shouldn't have come in summer, I thought. Perspiration began to run down my back and into my butt-crack.

Great! I was going to look just like those southern farmers you see in the movies: walking around with giant brown wet spots exuding from some of the most sacred parts of my body.

There were no cabs waiting, so I asked the guy sitting next to me about it.

"Taxicab?" he said, and gave me a look like I was obviously from New York City. "None too many of 'em around hea'. You could call and wait. Might be a spell."

I considered asking just how long a spell *was* in Mussel Shoals, but thought better of it.

"Wife's pickin' me up. We could drop you in town if you don' wanna wait."

Now, my mother always taught me *never* to ride with strangers. This guy talked a little funny, but he really didn't seem strange. I was desperate, and said, "That would be wonderful."

Then I asked if his car had air conditioning.

"Ain't no car, issa pickup." And he laughed good-naturedly. He didn't answer my question about the air, so I just assumed I shouldn't expect it. When the ride came, it was like something George C. Scott had driven in the movie *The Flim-Flam Man*.

There was a passel full of kids up front. At least I think they call them a passel down here. The man kissed his wife through the window, then walked around to the other side and climbed in.

I didn't want to appear as one of those dumb city slickers by asking where I was riding. I threw my two, new, beautiful pieces of luggage in the back and climbed aboard. I was a bit dismayed to find one of them had landed smack dab on top of something resembling excrement, but I sure didn't believe it could be, so I just held on and concentrated on seeing the sights.

What a sight it was to see. I don't think I have ever seen so many rusty tin roofs in all my life. There were tin roofs on shanty shacks and warehouses, on doghouses, and a lot of people houses as well. These people were real fond of tin, I soon realized.

The man hadn't asked where I was going. The truck just stopped in the middle of a bunch of old stores, many with boards on the windows. I heard him say, "Well, this is downtown. You have a good trip now, ya hea'!"

That was my cue to disembark. I wasted no time in doing so. As the truck left me in a cloud of noxious black smoke, I would for years come to swear that I had heard the old time actor Walter Brennan cackling somewhere in the background.

I saw the Motel sign a couple of blocks away, so I started walking toward it. The Internet said it had a pool and air conditioning, so I was making my way to it like a man dying of thirst in a barren desert. The problem was just that. I *was* dying of thirst after about twenty... well, maybe it was only ten paces. Flying always dehydrates me, and I had read stories of what happens when a person develops sunstroke. Not pretty, so I figured I'd better get out of the beating rays immediately.

Ahhh! I spotted what I had been searching for. It wasn't one of those cool, easy to see, lighted signs, so I almost missed it. It said BEER, and it was painted in canary yellow on a piece of old plywood standing up inside a window that looked like it hadn't been washed since "Sweet Home Alabama" had been played hourly on most radio stations America-wide in the early seventies.

I drug myself and my bags through the door, expecting as you would, that a bar would be cool inside, and have some patrons, too. *So much for expectations*, I thought

Behind the bar was one of the biggest black men I have ever seen. I mean he wasn't the tallest, but he was *really* big.

Sidling up to the bar, which was made of rough shipping pallets covered on top with some more of that old plywood, I sat. I immediately felt something poking my hamstring and looked down to see that the stool was made the same way. A bent nail had been pounded down almost all the way, and the head was scratching me. I tried to ignore the nail and chalked it up to atmosphere.

He looked at me and didn't say a word. *Not the friendly type*, I thought. No wonder business was slow. You see, I pride myself on being able to walk into nearly any commercial establishment and pick up on the reasons it is doing well, or poorly, at once. This place was *screaming* at me.

"I'd like a beer…please." I had looked at him closely, and then added the please as an afterthought. The Big man didn't look friendly, so I figured a little charm couldn't hurt.

He reached under the plywood and brought up a can. Now, I don't normally drink beer from cans. This one said, "Beer" in great big letters. It had no brewery name on it. I was sure he wasn't attempting to pass off an imitation, but I'd never seen beer like that before. Even if I had, it surely wouldn't have been my choice. I'm a micro-brew kind of guy. So I asked him what other kinds he had.

I will remember his first spoken words 'til my dying day. They so surprised me that I was speechless for a full five seconds, which was a first for me. He voice was deep and had a strange…shrill edge to it, like he was offended or something. And I was trying *very* hard *not* to offend him! As I said before, he was *really* Big.

"Ain't no utha!"

Now, I don't consider myself to be slow on the draw mentally, but this time anyone observing would have guessed differently.

"Okay..." I said masterfully.

He slid the can to me and said, "Six bits."

I had heard the term "two bits" when I was a kid. Some old timers used to say that...but six bits? It took my heat-stressed mind a moment to calculate.

He just glared. It seemed like *that* can of beer was the only one left in the whole wide world, and he didn't *want* to sell it to me.

Now I know cheap beer goes for about three bucks a six-pack. So this guy was clearing about a quarter on my transaction. Looking around the place and estimating his average traffic flow, I quickly calculated his monthly business income, before things like rent, air conditioning, and refrigeration. He was obviously cutting some corners there. His inflow was about three hundred seventy-five dollars. I had no idea what rent in this neighborhood was, but felt it would have to be conservative. So I guessed his net monthly was running about ninety bucks.

I wasn't going to ask him to start a tab. His scowl told me he wasn't really the trusting type. I opened my wallet, then glanced behind me nonchalantly to see that no one was there looking into my travel stash before I pulled out a twenty. I slid it across the bar to him and picked up the can. It was room temperature. "Do you have a cold one?" I asked.

He didn't say anything for another uncomfortable five or six seconds, then he shoved the bill back to me, and I got the message loud and clear. There was only *one* kind of beer here, and it came warm.

I thought his gesture meant he wanted me to leave, but he spoke up, relieving me of that somewhat astounding thought.

"Got anythin' smaller?" he asked.

I dug frantically in my pockets for loose change, then remembered my habit of shedding all my loose change before I go through airport security. I hate that buzzer and the looks people give you when you *finally* pull an errant penny from some unknown pocket you had completely forgotten about.

I must have had that deer in the headlights look I can get when I'm lost at a crossroads and am locked up in fear.

He pulled my twenty back, turned, and walked away from me, shaking that big wide neck. Well, it really looked more like three big truck inner tubes, stacked one on top of the other, not a neck at all. Maybe that's not the right analogy, but at the time...maybe the heat was getting to me...it looked just like three huge, stacked inner tubes.

I opened the beer, grimacing while he had his back turned, and slugged down about half the can. The carbonation burned my throat like other beer when you drink it that fast. It was wet. I was thirsty. By the time he had wrangled a table of decrepit old men playing checkers for proper change, I had the beer finished.

He counted out my change very professionally, laying it on the counter. I asked if I could trouble him for another. He looked at my pile of change, calculating quickly I could see, whether my purchase would force him to walk anywhere to make change for a second time. Satisfied, I could tell by the merest hint of a smile at one corner of his mouth, he said, "No trouble."

This time the deep voice had no shrill edge, and he pulled another can from under the bar—if you could call it a bar.

The room seemed to be getting hotter. Or maybe it was the pressure I had felt when he silently glared at me. Anyway, the next can actually felt a tad cooler than my hand. I opened it quickly and chugged down about a third of it.

"See, 'tain't ha'f bad when you open your throat like that," he said, smiling. The man had the whitest teeth you could imagine. They were perfectly aligned, and I knew instinctively that he had been born with the genes that made teeth like that naturally. This man had not had to suffer adolescence with a birdcage strangling his teeth, or the distasteful visits to the nazi cow orthodontist either. I found myself envying him slightly.

I had just visited my dentist for my regular clean and polish. I didn't dare smile. I felt inferior. Maybe the heat was getting to me.

He pulled up a stool and stayed near me so that he could just reach under the bar without moving his great frame anytime I needed a new can. It seemed I was already his best customer, and I didn't even know his name.

"I'm Jay." I held out my hand, which was another stupid move. If this guy had a mean streak, he could crush my hand in his big paw as easily as crushing one of those small bags of potato chips you get with your burger when you don't feel like springing extra for fries.

My hand was sticking out there like a turkey drumstick in front of a kennel of starving bluetick hounds, and I couldn't very well pull it back as an afterthought. He looked me in the eye for a moment, then took my hand and shook it politely. "It's a pleasure," he said in perfect English. "I'm John. But don't you *dare* ever call me big!"

I was astounded. Since getting off the plane, I had heard a constant dialect that was completely abnormal to my ears. I kept wanting to say, "What did you just say?" but knew better than to open my mouth. Someone could be insulting my heritage, and I would blindly nod rather than draw attention to the fact that I could understand only about half the words people were speaking. I could be in northern Scotland in one of those quaint little seaside villages with all the rock huts and pick up more passing conversation.

I was surprised because before he had spoken only the confusing and unrelenting southern jargon; now he was speaking clear as a bell. "Well, John, I'm happy to meet you, and I promise...." I almost said, "I will never call you Big." I quickly recovered and finished my sentence by saying, "I'll only have one more beer."

"You ain't drivin' are you?"

"No. I just need to walk another block to my motel."

"You stayin' at the Dixy Inn?"

"Yes!" I said, sure and confident of my Internet research.

"Well, if ya havin' to stay there, don't let 'em put you in room twelve!"

"What's wrong with room twelve, John?"

"I didn't say something was wrong with it! I just said don't let 'em put you in twelve!"

I could tell I wasn't getting any more out of him on *that* subject, so I changed the channel.

"You know, John, I could give you a few tips…business tips that would greatly increase your clientele and your profitability." I was beginning to feel the generic beer. Some people say that stuff is just like water. I can attest that it is *not*. After my fourth one, I was feeling like I could be an expert on just about anything.

John feigned interest, saying, "Oh?"

"Yes! For one thing, you need a cooler…to keep the beer cold. And another you need to get a better sign. I almost missed it the window is so dirty. And if you swept up, and knocked down the cobwebs from the ceiling, and painted those atrocious water spots, you would be a lot busier. There are other things, you know…the ones I mentioned are just the basics."

"Other things?" he said, smiling enigmatically, those big, perfectly white teeth glistening.

"Well sure, John…you could *look* happier. When I first came in here, you looked downright mean. That could scare off potential customers. I know you would like to be a lot busier, so I just thought I would tip you in the right direction."

"How do you know that?"

"Well, people go into business to make money…I don't mean to be insulting, but you must be starving on the meager profits from this place."

"Do I look like I'm starving?" He stood up so I could get a good look at his physique…if you could call it that.

I shook my head. "No. I have to admit you don't, John. But what I'm talking about is getting more people through that door!"

"Don' wan' no mo' people comin' in the door!"

There was that shrill edge again. How strange, I thought. His voice was beautiful and deep...you know, the James Earl Jones type of voice, yet sometimes it seemed on the edge of cracking.

When his voice did that, it made me extremely uncomfortable.

But it was his response that stopped me in my tracks. I froze for a moment thinking of the word abstract, because for me his response was glaringly so. I've never been too good at things abstract...I'm a nuts and bolts kind of guy. Give me a wrench and a loose nut, and I'll tighten it down.

Thinking of a business that didn't want more customers really didn't compute. So my flesh and blood computer just locked right up.

John must have seen that I was about to smoke a circuit breaker, so he explained his point of view in laymen's terms.

"You see, Jay, I got my pension. Three tours in 'Nam, two purple hearts, and a disability check for some shrapnel I'm still carrying. I don't need money. I *need* peace and quiet."

He spoke the word "need" as if he were a vampire saying, I *need* blood.

"I go home, and I got a list of honey do's that never ends. Whenever I accomplish one thing on the list, the wife adds two more. Most the stuff don't need doin' anyway. Hell, if I paint the house every year like my wife wants, then my poor neighbors get to feelin' bad 'cause they home lookin' worse off'n mine. I don't want to do them poor folk that way.

"That's just an example." John started in on that perfect English again. "I love my wife—she's a sweet woman.

One thing she does is listen to those evangelical radio shows all day. I can take a little of that...but *all* day?

"You see, I come here for my quiet time. I don't need any more money. If I get more customers, it won't be quiet anymore. Some of them will want a TV. I'll have to start working, which is *just* what I come here *not* to do.

"If I wash that window, more people will notice the sign. If I sweep the floor and paint, then more people will come back.

"You see those old boys playing checkers?"

I nodded my head.

"They are in the same boat as me. They are the *only* customers I need. All we want is our peace and quiet and no honey do's. You dig what I'm telling you?"

The stage curtain rose on a movie—a new movie I had never comprehended could exist. This was a private club. Somehow, I had been graced with acceptance. Honor flooded around me. I swam in bliss.

"Thanks for letting me drink here, John." Then I shut up. The silence was nice, in a strange sort of way. It was completely fresh to me.

I picked up that warm can, gulped the last swallow, and asked for another. I thought in wonderment, how much *better* the beer tasted now.

I figured I'd better not wear out my welcome. John began looking at me and then at the door. He wasn't a man of many words, and I surely didn't want him wasting some of his by asking me to leave. So after the fourth...or was it fifth beer, I nodded quietly, thanking him again in silence, grabbed my bags, and headed for the door.

Just as I opened it, and the afternoon heat hit me in the face like a brick, he said, "Don' go forgettin' what I tol' you about room twelve!"

I nodded again and departed.

CPSIA information can be obtained at www.ICGtesting.com
Printed in the USA
BVOW071142270113

311619BV00001B/4/P